THE GIFT OF GAB

THE GIFT OF GAB

Randall Ivey

Green Altar Books
Shotwell Publishing

The Gift of Gab
Copyright© 2024 by Randall Ivey

ALL RIGHTS RESERVED. No part of this publication may be reproduced, distributed, or transmitted in any form or by any means, including photocopying, recording, or other electronic or mechanical methods, or by any information storage and retrieval system without the prior written permission of the publisher, except in the case of very brief quotations embodied in critical reviews and certain other non-commercial uses permitted by copyright law.

This book is a work of fiction. Names, characters, businesses, organizations, places, events and incidents either are the product of the author's imagination or are used fictitiously. Any resemblance to actual persons, living or dead, events, or locales is entirely coincidental.

Produced in the Republic of South Carolina by
GREEN ALTAR BOOKS,
an imprint of Shotwell Publishing LLC
Post Office Box 2592
Columbia, So. Carolina 29202
www.ShotwellPublishing.com

Cover Design: Boo Jackson

ISBN: 978-1-963506-22-8

FIRST EDITION

10 9 8 7 6 5 4 3 2 1

Contents

The Gift Of Gab 1

The Bereaved 17

Mr. Aldon 35

A Death By The River 43

The Dead Will Provide 57

Mae Ola: A Remonstrance 71

Old Man's Burden 75

The Dark Garden 97

Miss Blitch Of Helton Avenue 117

Crow Boy 121

What A Jezebel Looks Like 143

In Spring The Sun Will Smell Like Roses 149

A Plinth Of Night 161

Landscape 177

About The Author 179

*For Jean and Paul Denman
and years of steadfast friendship
and support.*

Acknowledgments

These journals/websites were kind enough to offer some of these stories homes prior to this book:

Abbeville Institute: "Crow Boy," "Landscape," "Old Man's Burden," and "A Plinth of Night"

The Chiron Review: "A Death by the River"

The Dead Mule School of Literature: "Mae Ola: A Remonstrance," "Mr. Alton," and "What a Jezebel Looks Like"

Emrys Journal: "In Spring the Sun Will Smell Like Roses"

Still: The Journal: "The Gift of Gab"

The Gift of Gab

Used to be you couldn't go no place in Compton County without running into Miss Jenny DeGraffenreid.

I mean *no place*!

Flea market, grocery store, gas station, butcher's market, jewelry store, beauty shop, and church, of course.

The Methodist church.

For Miss Jenny, the Methodist faith was the only Christ-approved one in existence. (And here us Baptists thinking it was the closest thing to paganism this side of the Orient.)

Downtown too, naturally, where her and her old man run the pharmacy, Murray's Drugs, which they bought from Mr. T.J. Murray way back in 1969.

DeGraffenreid ain't a common name in Compton, then or now. That is because Miss Jenny's husband, Dr. Phillip DeGraffenreid, come to South Carolina all the way from Gadsen, Alabama, went to pharmacy school in Charleston, and set up shop here in Compton in the South Carolina upcountry. We all traded at Murray's Drugs because that's all they was then, before your Revcos and your Wal-Greens and such. And even after them establishments made their way to Compton, we *still* traded with the DeGraffenreids because our mamas and our daddies had and we had been friends with Jenny and Phillip all them years and had never made the acquaintance of Mr. Revco or Mr. Walgreen. We got our prescriptions at Murray's, naturally, but also our baseball cards, our smokes, our soda pops, our funny books and greeting cards, our rasslin tickets, and just about everything else. About the only things Murray's didn't sell were automobiles and beachfront property, and I'm sure if Miss Jenny could have arranged it, they would have carried *them* as well.

Nine years ago, Dr. Phillip passed from heart trouble, and heartbroke herself over it, Miss Jenny decided to shut down Murray's (they kept the original owner's name all them years out of respect to Mr. T.J. and it being a well-knowed brand in town since 1935). That was an event, truly. It made the radio and the newspaper, and the Chamber of Commerce thowed Miss Jenny a big party at the National Guard Armory to thank her and Dr. Phillip and to wish her well.

But Miss Jenny did not just fade away, as General McArthur said old soldiers do. If anything, she become more visible about town. Her and the doctor never had no children of their own, for what reason we never found out nor had the nerve to ask, it not being our business or nothing.

"I'd die if I stayed home and done nothing," Miss Jenny declared once when asked how come she didn't slow down and enjoy her retirement. "I'd just die!"

And slow down she did not. She was already a fixture in the Methodist church, where she volunteered for everything, but she joined the Lions Club, the Civitans, the Lady Elks, the Clemson Booster Club, the Gamecock Club (she had always pulled for both teams so as not to make nobody upset and lose customers), and any other group that would have her. And they all did, seeing how much money she had and was willing to donate. She was a millionaire several times over, thanks to her and Dr. Phillip's hard work and prudent habits and, of course, they never had younguns to raise.

The only thing she did not give money to – was adamant about not giving to – was the public library. Wouldn't do it, even though the folks there begged and pleaded and sent note after note asking for donations. She did not like books and never had. She took pride in the fact she had never read a book all the way through in her whole entire life, except for The Bible, and truth be told she only skimmed through that one, having the Methodist preacher do the rest of the work for her. Why read when they was so much else to do and see, so many new people to meet, so much talking to get done?

Talking!

Now that was Miss Jenny's real love and her favorite thing to do in all the world. She could talk the ears off a corncob if given the chance, and she would talk to anybody, since, as the saying (and must surely have been wrote expressly for Miss Jenny), she never met a stranger. Or if she did meet one, they wasn't a stranger for long. She'd talk to a youngun, a man, a woman, a cat, a dog, a bush, a stop sign, a go sign, whatever might happen to be in front of her at the time. She'd talk to the Queen of England or the foreman at the junkyard. *Talk* now, not listen, for she did not do much of the latter. It was all The Jenny DeGraffenreid show once she got started. You get engaged talking to her, and you couldn't hardly get away from her! "One more thing," she'd say after talking to you for a half hour or more, but that minute found a way to stretch into forty minutes, and before you knew it, your whole night is shot. She could outtalk the preacher in the pulpit and the politician at the pork-pull.

"Miss Jenny," someone asked her once, "I bet you talk in your sleep, don't you?"

"Hon," Miss Jenny replied, "if I could tell you that, I wouldn't be sleeping, now would I?

It must be said that while Miss Jenny did not discriminate against who it was she talked to, she did have a clear preference for men. Liked 'em a great deal and insisted they hug her before she talked to them and after, and if the man wasn't careful, and perhaps even if he was, he might find Jenny's hand sneaking down his back and below his belt and pinching a substantial portion of his rungunkus. The man would jump, and Jenny would laugh, just like a youngun that's got away with something it ought not to have done in the first place.

But we loved the old gal – love her still, oh yes. No need to put this in the past tense of things, although we don't see her like we used to.

She was a gabber for sure but cute as a button in her own way, short and bowl-legged as a sailor and naïve as a little youngun. You could tell her almost anything, and she would almost always believe you. Tell the moon's made of green cheese, and she'd wonder aloud what crackers went the best with it. Tell her they's a ghost haunting the Compton courthouse, and she'd fret about how many meals a day it got. And such as that. We laughed at her, yes, but with her too, because she was good-natured and could take a joke at her own expense, and we loved her to death for how good-hearted she was and open with her pocketbook when it come to good causes around town. Nobody else even come close to Miss Jenny.

About five years ago, big news come to our little town – the opening of The Pancake Palace! Yes, in little old Compton, South Carolina! They had them everywhere else but here, so when they finally opened up here, it stayed filled up for nearly a month. You couldn't get a table lessen you went some unearthly hour of the morning, and even then it wasn't guaranteed. Well, Jenny DeGraffenreid go in, no trouble, because that is the sort of person she is, determined, head-strong, and refusing to take no for an answer. Some folks just got up and give her their seat after she had them froze good with all her talk. They wanted to get away from that as fast as they could, especially when she reminisced about Dr. Phillip and got all teared-up and sentimental. Lord, who could turn down an old woman when she gets to crying? Nobody – lessen they made completely of rock.

So she become as much a fixture at Pancake Palace as she was at the Methodist church and even more, since the church only met three or four times a week and Pancake Palace was opened twenty-four hours a day, seven days a week, fifty-two weeks a year, including Christmas and Thanksgiving. She didn't always order something to eat. Sometimes she just got her a cup of coffee in her booth sipping it for hours, for what she wanted more than a pancake was another person to talk to – anybody would do, friend or stranger, young or old, black or yellow or green, Methodist or Baptist or atheist. It didn't matter. She just did not want to go home to that lonely house of hers, the one her and Dr. Phillip built all them years ago and lived in till he passed. She's a people person, Miss Jenny, not a reader of books or watcher of TV. And nine times out of ten she could find somebody at Pancake Palace to listen to her, even if it was just a waiter or a cook. She'd get there late too, sometimes after ten or eleven, and folks close to her worried about her being out after dark and so late. So much meanness goes on now, even in Compton, and it wouldn't take nothing for somebody to come up and knock Miss Jenny on the head as she was leaving her car for the Palace or the Palace for her car. Knock her out and take her money. Or goodness knows what's worse. But Jenny wouldn't mind them and done what she wanted. She figured she was old and widowed and deserved some company. The staff at Pancake Palace done some looking after her, but they had their jobs to do, and sometimes they had to pry theirselves loose from her since she had so much to say about so many things. "Lord, here comes Miss Jenny," they'd say when they seen her Cadillac pull up and slide into a parking place. "Better act like you busy or she'll talk your ear off." They liked Miss Jenny good enough for the most part. She give a generous tip and told a funny joke or story (sometimes more than once to the same person the same night), and hard as it may be to believe, sometimes things got slow and quiet even at The Pancake Palace, so the young folks welcomed the company even of a gabby old woman.

About a year ago, The Pancake Palace hired a new cook, a boy named Rocky Seward, a big old boy who had spent some time in prison, off and on, for this and that. Not a real bad boy necessarily, just one who tended to let other people do his thinking for him, and nine times out of ten, they made the wrong decision. He had a wife and couple of younguns and needed a job when he got out of the pokey. He had done some short order cooking all over Compton and elsewhere since he was a boy. He had been in the service too, and between that and prison had collected an impressive array of tattoos upon hisself, all the way from his stout ankles to his thick neck. He was a walking wall of graffiti, with all kinds of shapes drawed onto his body – skeleton keys, fierce-looking spiders, a palm tree, a lady's face, and some things that was tough to make out or that was covered by his clothes. (It must be a rule of employment at The Pancake Palace that you have, one, done some time in a South Carolina penitentiary, two, you smoke cigarettes like they was going out of style, and three, you got a good portion of yourself brightened up by ink. Rocky met all three requirements. With his height and his muscles and his tats and his low-slung forehead and his short, jet-black hair, he looked like something Dr. Frankenstein might have put together one night with spare parts in the laboratory.)

He was friendly enough, though not a master of the English language, not much of a talker in general. He nodded and spoke when you come in and left and sometimes attempted a joke that at least made him laugh. Otherwise, the most you might get out of him if you asked him how he was would be a "Ah 'ight." But Miss Jenny seemed to bring out something in him nobody else could, as him and her become especially buddy-like. If she called for him because of a problem with her order – her pancakes was burnt, her coffee was cold – he'd leave the grill and come see about her, and they'd get into a chitchat that moved far beyond the menu items at The Pancake Palace. She'd tell her story of woe, of missing Dr. Phillip and living alone in a lonely old house with no younguns of her own to comfort her, and he'd tell hissen, and hissen was worse, filled as it was with time in jail and folks that had used him and lied to him and such, and now he was just scraping by trying to make a living for hisself and a wife and two younguns on a Pancake Palace paycheck. Jenny'd listen to all this with tears in her eyes. She is a tender-hearted sort, always looking out for the other fellow, always worried somebody's doing without a meal or a warm place to lay down or a good set of teeth. She give and give and give, and all she wanted back was somebody to listen to her talk. And Rocky Seward done that when he could, so she made sure to slip him a five or ten spot when the manager wasn't looking.

Almost forgot. They's another requirement you must have, should you ever go wanting to work at The Pancake Palace. You cannot own your own automobile. You may or may not have a driver's license (and lots of 'em don't on account of all their DUIs), but you will more than likely NOT have a car to drive and therefore must depend on somebody else to get you back and forth to work, your mama or daddy, your boyfriend or girlfriend, even your teenage youngun. And if none of them is available to help you out, you just walk to and fro, sometimes miles, sometimes in the pitch dark or night or early morning, sometimes in the gushing rain or floating snow.

Such was the case with Rocky Seward. Him and his wife didn't have a car because they could not afford the payments or the insurance. Seems like most of the money they made went to hiding their skin with tattoos. Therefore, they had to hitch to wherever they went. (Rocky's wife cleaned houses in town.) Rocky was stout enough to do the walking if he had to, but he lived in the Beaslap community, some fifteen, twenty miles from The Pancake Palace, so it was not practical or safe to walk. He got rides where he could, sometimes from the store's general manager, Miss Rita Spence, most time from the other help.

One night, though, there come a dilemma. Miss Spence was sick in bed with the flu and Rocky's regular ride had not called in and could not be found by telephone, so Rocky was stuck as far as finding a ride home that night. None of the other staff on duty that night had cars, so that was out, and there was no dependable taxi service in Compton. He was stuck. That is till Miss Jenny DeGraffenreid showed in her big ol' Cadillac and come in with her big ol' pocketbook (the size of a suitcase really) and settled into a booth. It was near the end of Rocky's shift. He seen Miss Jenny arrive and grinned.

"You having your usual, Miss Jenny? Raisin toast and your bacon light and crispy?"

Miss Jenny giggled like a girl and said, "You know me too good, Rocky Top." That was her nickname for him.

Rocky went about preparing Miss Jenny's meal very carefully, making sure there were no lumps in her grits nor shells in her scrambled eggs. He took the plate to her hisself and stood watching to make sure she was satisfied.

"Good?" he asked at some point, anxious for her to be happy.

"Real good, Rocky Top!" she told him. "Thank you, sir!"

"You welcome."

He seen his chance then.

"Miss Jenny, I was wondering…. I hate to be a bother and all… but…I ain't got no way home this evening, and I was wondering kindly like…if…. Well, I wouldn't bother you for nothing in the world, but you always so good-hearted and giving and such to folks, and…."

Miss Jenny sat listening, a piece of buttered toast in one hand, a mug of coffee in the other. She decides to help him out right then, put him out of his misery of trying to put words together in a meaningful way, for Rocky Seward was no master-tongue with the English language, nor no other kind of language for that matter.

"You need me to give you a ride home, Rocky Top?"

"Yessum. That's what I was coming to eventually."

"Uh huh. And where is it you live?"

"Beaslap."

"Oh that's right. You done told me that before."

"Yes ma'am."

"Beaslap's a right far piece out, ain't it?"

"Yes ma'am. I'd be happy to give you gas money, Miss Jenny."

Jenny sat and thought, then said, "You don't have to do that. I'll take you home. But can I finish my coffee first? It's good to the last drop, and I don't want to miss none of it!" She made herself laugh, quoting that old coffee commercial, and Rocky, not exactly sure what was funny, laughed too, happy as he was to know he now had a ride home.

Miss Jenny took her time with her coffee, indeed enjoying it down to the dregs. Then, when she'd paid her bill, the two of them were off, and what a sight they must have made on the way out of The Pancake Palace! Her, short and stubby and, on account of her bowled legs, rocking back and forth like a youngun's play-purty, him, tall and stiff and straight like the insides of his clothes was weighed down with atomic bombs and he had to be real careful walking anywheres for fear he'd set hisself off.

Now what happened between the time Miss Jenny got Rocky Seward to Beaslap and made it back to Compton has been the subject of much speculation. Many mouths have contributed to its telling. First off, if any of Miss Jenny's good friends had knowed what she had agreed to do, they would have skint her alive – her a rich old widow lady traipsing around in the dark of night and giving a stranger a ride all the way to Beaslap!

"They could knock you on your head, Jenny, and take every dime you got," they would have said to her.

"They could kill you! Just like that! And not think a thing about it. You know what meanness goes on today!"

And in being confronted so, Jenny would have said, "But that Rocky's a nice boy! He's always good to me. Always gets my eggs and bacon *just* right!" (Which would have made her friends roll their eyes and rubbed their noggins.)

Beaslap, South Carolina, is no place for anybody to be out and about at night, young or old, rich lady or poor boy from The Pancake Palace. It was wild the day the Good Lord made it, and it has stayed wild to this day. It has a cursed feeling to it. People have died in its woods – hunters looking for deer and young girls looking for deer hunters. People have seen coyotes there, claim haints wander the woods hunting for ingredients to make their devilish stews. People do live there, black folks and white, good people, but spread out from each other, a smattering of houses here, another smattering there. Rocky Seward and his wife lived in a double-wide trailer off to theirselves far up an old gravel road that was almost covered over by fir trees and spruces. They was cut off from the world in a way.

Jenny found that out during the twenty-minute drive south into all that darkness. Nothing stirred out yonder! And they only had the moon and Miss Jenny's headlights to guide them along. The deeper they got into Beaslap, the more Miss Jenny's stomach turned and twisted. Rocky didn't turn out to be much company. He sat quiet beside her and only spoke to give Jenny directions. The road seemed to go on forever.

"You sure you don't live in North Carolina, Rocky?" Miss Jenny asked him. "This sure is a good piece out."

That made Rocky laugh, but he didn't say nothing else 'til they got to a point in the long road when his arm flew up and he pointed.

"Right yonder, Miss Jenny!" he said. "You turn here." And Jenny let out a long breath of relief, not caring if Rocky heard her or not. She turned and began the long climb up the Sewards' driveway, all closed over with spruces and pines like most of Beaslap, her Caddy rocking and knocking over gravel till she had to slow down the rest of the way, arriving at last at the double-wide, whose front windows was lit up orange with lamp light.

It concerned Jenny that Rocky Seward and his missus lived so far back from the main road. It got her to wondering what he done with his time when he wasn't raising pancakes off the griddle at The Palace. The first thing that come to mind was drugs. What if Rocky was a drug dealer who had led her all the way down yonder for The Lord knew what? The warning words of her friends come back loud and clear to her in the dark with her motor running and big ol' Rocky Seward lunging a bit towards her. Her mouth turned dry, and she felt sweat begin to run under her arms and the back of her neck.

"Miss Jenny, I sure do thank ye!" Rocky told her, his face close enough to hers that he could have kissed her if he wanted to.

"You welcome, Rocky," Miss Jenny said.

"I'd be happy to pay ye."

"No, no, Rocky! That's fine. I'm happy to have done it. Now –"

Rocky cut her off, something not many done to Jenny DeGraffenreid when she was talking. Fact of business, it's nothing *nobody* has ever done. "Why don't you come on in the house and say hey to my wife? She's heard all about you. Dying to meet you!"

"Oh no, hon. Thank you, but no. I reckon I best be getting back to Compton and all. It's getting right late."

But Rocky had got into his head the idea that Jenny was going to walk into that double-wide and meet Johnna, his wife, and like a lot of simple-minded folks do, he wasn't going to give up till he got his way. He insisted and insisted, like a youngun begging for something for Christmas, and Jenny's nerves go so tore up listening to him insist, she figured the only way to stop him was to give in. So she give in, knowing she shouldn't, and it just tickled Rocky to death, so much so that he led Jenny by the arm into his very humble abode – very humble.

It was as cramped a place as Jenny had ever seen, whose walls she swore moved inward as she stood and looked at them. She could have swore the place was shrinking right in front of her eyes. Two lamps burned on low tables across the floor from each other, giving off enough light so that Jenny could see a floor that hadn't been picked up in weeks. They was newspapers and magazines throwed about, dirty dishes and glasses laying up under them, and a funny smell hung over it all. Well, more than one smell. A mix of smells all got up together to make one ugly cloud. If she stood there long enough, Jenny could piece them out individually – cigarette smoke first and foremost, and she was sure there was alcohol and…well, she didn't want to think about the rest of what made up that smell. And just like somebody was reading her mind then, she heard squeals from across the floor and seen a playpen there with two younguns in it, both naked except for plastic diapers. It was dark in the trailer, but that didn't keep her from seeing that both the babies had dirty faces. They seen Jenny and grinned and reached out for her. Everything in the house was dirty, it looked like, and she made sure to be careful not to touch nothing and hoped she would not be offered nowhere to sit down. She decided she wouldn't touch nothing there, with her hand or her rear end, for all the gold in Fort Knox. They was no telling what was on it. She turned from the babies and seen Johnna, Mrs. Rocky, on the couch, the biggest piece of furniture in the room, watching a TV that stretched almost the whole of one wall. The program blared. They was gunshots and hollering. Johnna's face lit up as soon as her and Jenny made eye contact. She was a big gal, every bit Rocky's match, not so much fat as big-boned. She had black hair and not many teeth, and one cuff of her blue jeans was rolled up far enough on her stout leg to show a tattoo there, although Jenny didn't have enough light at the moment to make out the design. She had them on her arms too, both of them, bright snakes of ink that run up into her shirt sleeves and disappeared.

"Hey!" the girl hollered and come up off the couch lickety-split. She stomped right over to Jenny, paying Rocky no mind, and took her in a bear hug, like Jenny was her long-lost grandma.

"You must be Miss Jenny!" she said after the fact, and all Jenny could do was nod her little white head against the big gal's bosom, hoping the message got through. It must have, for Johnna went on: "Heard so much about ye! And ever bit of it good!" She released Jenny from her grip and smacked her three times in a row with three big ol' sloppy kisses then turned loose.

The Gift of Gab

"You a sweetheart!" she hollered in Jenny's face, the smell of liquor and cigarettes and cough medicine all mixed together in her breath and singeing Jenny's eyebrows. "Bringing my Rocky back on home to me."

Jenny laughed. "Yes. Pleased to do it. I call him 'Rocky Top,' by the way."

Johnna laughed like a horse, just neighed, and grabbed Jenny again and said, "That's just perfect! That's what I'm going to call him from now on. Rocky Top!" Then she begun to sing the famous song of the same name. Or done her best to.

Normally, Jenny would have loved meeting somebody new, would have talked this girl's ear off for an hour or two, if not longer. Would have asked her about anything and everything – about who her kin was and where she growed up, where she went to church, and all such as that. But not that night. That night she wanted to say hey and get gone, get in her car and get back to Compton, promising the Lord all the way back that she wouldn't never give another stranger a ride home, lessen He ordered her to Hisself in a voice she could not mistake as no other's but His. Her hosts, such as they was, however, was thinking otherwise. They wanted Jenny to stay so they could entertain her in some way. They offered her a glass of tea, a slice of pie, a bottle of beer (when they should have knowed better in the first place but reckoning that the Methodists was a bit looser in their habits.) And their younguns just squealed and hollered at the bars of the playpen, putting their hands through like they meant to fetch Jenny into the pen with them and get her as dirty as they was, pressing their nasty faces into the bars too, showing off their toothless mouths. At each offer, Jenny shook her head. She shook her head so much she got right swimmy-headed and had to stop. She thanked them for their hospitality. She wished them a good night. And she edged her little self out the door, but not before Johnna could grab her one more time and crush her to her person and holler out, "You my heart, Miss Jenny DeGravelreid! Yes, you are!"

In her car, Jenny hoped and prayed she could find her way back to Compton, not having Rocky's directions no more to help her.

The Good Lord was with her. She made it home without an incident and went straight to her bed, still in her clothes, and laid down shaking, like somebody who has come *this* close to a terrible, terrible accident. She couldn't sleep. All she could do was think about what a mess Rocky Seward's house was. She brought her fist up to her mouth and bit lightly into it. She began crying, worried about them nasty younguns in that nasty house and amazed that in a rich country like the United States of America, people still had to live like that. She swore to herself that she would not talk about what all she had seen down yonder in Beaslap, that it was Rocky Seward's business and not hers nor nobody else's.

But Compton, South Carolina, is a little ol' place, and people saw things that night and heard things later on and eventually made things up. Most folks wrote it all off as Miss Jenny just being Miss Jenny, doing for others like she always had. But they's folks had it out for Jenny DeGraffenreid – and for different reasons. Some was just jealous of her money, plain and simple. They didn't have nothing theirself and resented them what did. They shiftless types that would druther tear down the other fellow than spend that time and that energy to build their own self up. Others had plenty of their own, but not as much as Jenny and held it against her. They was some that thought it not a bit fair Jenny and Dr. Phillip had come to Compton from someplace so far off as Alabama and done so good. They thought she throwed her money around just for show and in their heart of hearts hoped she would fail at something – have the Stock Market crash around her or have her broker run out of town with everything or something else just as terrible.

So it was no surprise when the story of the night Miss Jenny drove Rocky Seward to Beaslap got changed and twisted up and told the wrong way by folks that wasn't there and only wanted to say something bad about somebody good. In the most common version that went around, Miss Jenny not only went into Rocky Seward's trailer to say hey, she stayed there the whole night! She accepted their offer of alcohol and threw back several shot glasses of Jim Beam and chased 'em down with Pabst Blue Ribbon and jiggers of tequila. Pretty soon she was as high as a kite. Her and Mr. and Mrs.

Seward, both of them just as snockered as she was, took off most of their clothes and danced in circles around the trailer like a trio of wild youngsters – and all in front of their baby boys!

They was variations to this account, but that is the story that got around most widely. Who started it? Nobody knows. Perhaps somebody at The Pancake Palace who never got to wait on Miss Jenny and therefore never got one of her good tips. Perhaps Rocky Seward hisself, for whatever reason. The fact is, it got around, and some folks believed it and told others and so on. They believed it because they wanted to believe it, because it's good to feel like you better than somebody else who's got more than you do, who's done more than you, even if the feeling last only a little bit.

Miss Jenny was the last to hear all this talk, of course. A friend who caught wind of it, went especially to Jenny's house, set her down in a comfortable chair, and told her everything, all the talk that was going around Compton that had Miss Jenny acting like a drunk beast in the wilds of Beaslap. This friend said after hearing it, Jenny's mouth fell open. The blood drained out of her face. Her hands shook. Then she busted out good in tears and fell against the back of the chair. She cried harder than she had since Dr. Phillip passed, maybe harder, since now it was her hard-earned reputation getting killed in the mouths of enemies and strangers. It never occurred to her anybody could talk about her that way or think those kinds of things. She was right child-like that way. And after all she done! She believed everybody had good intentions and that anytime she done a good deed with her money or said a kind word to a stranger or give a poor working boy a ride home, it was marked up not only in the accounts of Heaven but in the hearts of her neighbors. Now the truth was out. In the eyes of Compton, she was nothing more than a silly old rich lady, and that it was okay to make fun of and lie about. It didn't matter how much money she had give to this or to that or that she had a perfect attendance at the Methodist church. In fact, all that made it worse. Jenny's friend, the bearer of the bad news, said it was like Jenny just shrunk into that lounge chair, just shrunk into it and was no more.

And fact of business, that's when we all lost Jenny DeGraffenreid. Not literally. She didn't pass or nothing. She just…withdrawed from everything. Give up all she loved – the clubs and the auctions and the meetings and the events downtown and The Pancake Palace, of course – everything but the Methodist Church, which she still attends faithfully on Sundays and Wednesdays but without lingering afterwards or doing anything extry. Once the service is done, she's gone back to her house, not to come out again, lessen it's to keep a doctor's appointment. Otherwise, she's a hermit, determined not ever again to expose herself to hateful talk and gossip. Her friends go to see her, which is her sole comfort now, and that and her love of the Lord, and to one of them friends she once remarked, bitter as coffee grounds, "It just don't pay to be good to nobody."

The Bereaved

Ort not to have surprised nobody the way Debbie Lynn acted at her uncle's funeral. It sure didn't surprise me, because I have always knowed the truth about her: The girl is crazy!

I say "girl" when fact of business Debbie Lynn Fulton is nearly sixty years old. But she so acts like a youngun, and always has, that it is sometimes easy to forget how old she really is.

She ain't growed up. And never will. Ain't never held a steady job. Don't want a job. Too lazy. Would druther just set around the house and smoke or sniff something to get high. She's got a buddy, Wanda, who's rotted out every tooth in her head doing that crystal meth, and she brings the both of 'em things to get messed up on. And I have heard more than one story about how Debbie Lynn and Wanda have gone out high as kites in public and made total fools out of theirselves.

And men. Debbie Lynn loves to chase after men, and ain't a-one of 'em she's caught worth catching. Like this new one. Or should I say old one? Lewis Brown. From Gaffney. Which right there tells you he ain't much to begin with. All he does is use Debby Lynn for sex and money and everything like that. Plays games with her. And I don't mean Monopoly. I mean he makes her think he loves her then pulls the rug out from under her and takes up with some other poor, dumb piece of white trash.

"I'm done with him," she says. "He won't get this piece of ass no more."

Then a day or two later he'll call her and she'll go running back up yonder to him like a hound dog being whistled home.

I said oncet, "Debbie Lynn, I thought you was through with him."

And she said, "We just good friends is all. We just gone talk on the phone now and then. And now and then, I might let him take me out to dinner."

Shit!

It'd be *her* taking *him* out to eat if anything. All he's after is her money and everything like that. He's waiting for when she starts drawing Jimmy's Social Security. Jimmy. Debbie Lynn's dead husband. Now that was a good boy. A saint almost, if ever they was a saint in the state of South Carolina. Had to be one to put up married to Debbie Lynn all them years and getting nothing back from her but grief and the sound of that big mouth twenty-four hours a day. She treated him like dirt. Dirt! Thowed off on him. Even said oncet she couldn't wait till he died, 'cause then she would be one rich bitch! And Lord knows he done his best to accommodate her that way. Had every disease knowed to man. Seemed to attract 'em or collect 'em. Like his bloodstream went around hunting for something terrible to take hold of it. Sugar. Heart attack. Cancer. Lung cancer and cancer of the prospect. You name it, Jimmy had it at one time or another and sometimes at the same time. He'd been to the hospital so much, it's a wonder they didn't rename it for him. The only one he lacked was the Old Timey's, and I feel sure if he had lived a little longer he would have caught that one too. But he never complained. No sir. Not oncet.

He was good to Debbie Lynn, and she was so hateful to him. He helped her raise her onliest child, Michael, was the onliest daddy Michael ever knowed, since his real one, Danny, nothing but puretee trash, run off the second Michael come into the world. And when Michael died from a accidental gunshot wound, it was Jimmy what took it the hardest and nearly grieved hisself to death, not that Debbie Lynn didn't grieve too. She did. But Jimmy took it extry hard it seems, 'cause Michael was the onliest son he ever had. All his other children, from another wife, was girls. And I believe Michael, at least when he was a boy, give Jimmy the real, pure love Debbie Lynn held back from him and everything like that. Michael give Jimmy Fulton's life meaning.

Anyway, Jimmy had the one last heart attack that took him out for good, and Michael had been dead for nearly five years. Debbie Lynn had nothing left, or at least she thought so, so she just went wild. Fifty-something years old, almost sixty, and durn if she didn't think she was sixteen again. Going out to clubs. Drinking and dancing all night. Taking up with strange men. It got so bad her church, Gospel Truth Baptist, who got wind from somebody about Debbie Lynn's goings on, held an emergency meeting about it, about whether or not to ask Debbie Lynn to leave, which, of course, didn't set well at all with Debbie Lynn.

"Ain't none of their damn business what I do the other six days of the week long as I'm in that pew on Sunday."

I said, "But they don't see it that way. To them you sinning."

Debbie Lynn thowed up her face and pinched her lips real tight. "Ain't no telling what they do behind closed doors," she said, like she was singing a chorus of Charlie Rich.

And eventually, she met this Lewis Brown in Gaffney, who ain't nothing but a nasty old man that uses women. Debbie Lynn showed me a picture of him on her phone, and he ain't nothing at all to look at. Not a bit. Just a old man – white-headed and rusty. I could smell the old and the nasty on him right through the phone.

"What is it you see in him, Debbie Lynn?" I asked her.

"He's good to me. We have a good time together."

Shit!

He takes from her is what he does and don't give very much back.

Like last Christmas. He give her a teddy bear that he got for two dollars at the Dollar General and a newspaper insert cookbook that didn't cost him nothing.

Now tell me: what woman wouldn't go for that?

Me and her mama, Bertie Mae, was worried about her, naturally. She was out of control. She didn't have nothing good going on for her, nothing to fall back on. No job. No insurance. Nothing. What money she had she got from Bertie Mae, who, fact of business, didn't really have it to give, living like she was off Social Security and a little pension from Compton Mill. But Bertie just gives and gives, to her younguns and her grandyounguns, whether she's got it or not. Just hands it out to this one and that one. She's not so much generous as she is...well...stupid.

Anyway, me and Bertie Mae, for the last two or three years, had been helping out part time with our brother Emory. His wife Doris had got down real low in her back and on top of that had a mini-stroke. She pretty much couldn't get around or do much for herself no more. Was confined mostly to her chair and her bed. And Emory had us come in from morning to noon to help out with things. We cleaned and washed and cooked some and everything like that. Mostly though we tended to Doris – got her out of bed, fed her breakfast and dinner, and took her back and forth to the bathroom and everything like that. And Emory give us a little something every week, usually fifty dollars a-piece, which Bertie Mae would then turn right around and give Debbie Lynn or somebody else with a hand out and itching.

Well, last fall we got some bad news. Emory was sick with cancer of the colon and the liver. Just come out of nowhere, it seems. Emory was always a big ol' boy, always coming and going and doing, strong as a ox, even as a old man, just like our daddy, Bert McMillan. He had big old hands and a stout constitution. Even after his heart operation he could lift Doris and take her here and there and do most everything else, even though he wasn't 'pose to. And I can't help but think it was his doing for Doris what brought on the cancer and everything like that. One Saturday he got to complaining about his belly bothering him and being stopped up and everything like that, and the next day he was so weak he couldn't hardly get out of the bed. His daughter Lisa and her husband got him to Spartanburg the day after that, and turns out he had a liver infection. But after they poked and prodded and peeked some more, they found out it was a whole lot worser than that. It was cancer. Stage four. It had begun in the colon and spread to the liver. Stage four. Three weeks. Three months. Three years. They didn't know exactly how long he would last. But the fact was he wouldn't be able to handle Doris no more, not weak as he was, so me and Bertie Mae got to pulling longer hours or leaving the house for a while then coming back. Emory's son Will, who teaches school in Compton, would come and stay with his Mama and Daddy at night, and Lisa, the daughter, would fill in what holes in the time was left. But after a while me and Bertie Mae got good and tuckered. We ain't younguns no more, neither of us. I am seventy-six. Bertie Mae is seventy-eight. And they ain't a bone in neither of us wants to act right these days. Bone nor organ. You get to a certain age and you wake up and try to get out of bed, and everything in you starts to pop and crack and creak till you wonder if you'll be able to make it up at all without falling into a pile of your own rusty bones right there on the bedroom floor. Bertie Mae has a bad back. I got trouble with both my knees. We knowed we couldn't pull no ten or twelve hour shift at Emory's and still be able to stand upright at the end of the day. We tried it. It didn't work. We'd leave Emory's house hunched over like a pair of go-rillas.

So we got the idea: get Debbie Lynn to come over and set with Emory and Doris in the afternoon till Will got there and took over. She wasn't working nowhere else at the time. All she was doing was wasting time over at Bliley Place, the old folks home where Mama used to stay before we put her in the nursing home. She could make herself a little money and maybe rein herself in some, cut down on that running around and man-chasing and everything like that. We run the notion by Emory. He said, "Good idea, good idea" and raised up his thumb. And me and Bertie Mae breathed some in relief.

Debbie Lynn agreed to it too, though not whole hearted like we wished she had. She's got a lazy streak in her a mile wide and honest to goodness thinks she's too good to work and everything like that. Don't know who in the world told her she was a queen and a lady of leisure, but the idea sets in her head like a stubborn old hound dog and won't move. But she took on the afternoon shift, one to six, and seemed to do good enough. Onliest thing was she'd get around Emory and Doris and start talking about Lewis Brown and wouldn't quit talking about him and would say the same things over and over like they was fresh to the ears of her hearers, which they wasn't, of course. "Me and him's just friends. We talk on the phone. I let him take me to dinner. That's all. We ain't nothing but friends." And then she'd turn around a few minutes later and say the very same thing. Got so bad Emory begged her to take him to bed to lay down so he wouldn't have to hear no more of it. Told me and Bertie Mae one time he wished the cancer would go ahead and take him so he wouldn't have to hear no more about that Lewis Brown this and Lewis Brown that. He was being silly, naturally, but he had a point, one we just about all could see and agree to. It was like a fever or a virus had got hold of Debbie Lynn, a disease by the name of Lewis.

"We done. We broke up," she said one day for about the fifty-'leventh time, and here we'd thought they'd *been* broke up for a while.

"Again?"

"He can find hisself another piece of ass, 'cause this one's moving on to bigger and better things."

"What happened this time, Debbie Lynn? What did he do now?"

"Called me a whore. Right in front of his own daughter. Right in front of Theresa."

"And what did you say?"

"I said if I was a whore then I was his whore, and if he didn't appreciate what this whore had to give, she would take it someplace else. And that's just what I'm a-doing."

And then durn if not a couple days later she'd be back telling how her and Lewis had made up and he wanted her to move up to Gaffney with him and everything like that.

Shit!

I never had met a more mixed-up human being in all my life.

Well, winter come on and things with Emory got worse. He wouldn't eat nothing hardly, and if he tried, he couldn't keep it down no time. Lived pretty much on them protein drinks you get in a can. Will and 'em did manage to get Emory up to Gatlinburg, Tennessee, for one last time, just before Christmas. Emory loved Gatlinburg better than any other place on the face of this earth. He really did. Better than the beach. Good thing they done it too, took him, 'cause he just got worser and worser. Spent Christmas Day in bed. New Year's too. He slept too much. Got his days and nights flipped backwards. Will, who was still staying with his mama and daddy at night in case they needed help, said Emory would get wide awake in the middle of the night and holler down the hallway: "Hey boy! Hey! What's going on in here? I want to know what the hell's going on in this house." Will would trudge down yonder to see what his daddy wanted, usually a glass of water or help to go tee-tee. Will'd help his daddy and go back to bed, and it wouldn't be five minutes later Emory'd holler again: "Hey boy! What's going on in here?" And it'd start all over again and everything like that.

Got to where nobody in that house was getting much sleep, so Will and 'em decided to take their daddy to Spartanburg and put him in something called "respite care." Not hospice. Respite. They put him in a big room, big and nice as a hotel suite, and they treated him just royal. Least that's what Will and 'em said. They didn't take Emory there to die but to rest, so they could all get some rest. But Emory got it in his head they did take him there to die, and he got right ugly about it and accused Will and Lisa and 'em of such a thing, told 'em to get out of that room and not to come back no more. Pretty much raised up in his bed he was so upset with 'em. It was the cancer talking, of course. Otherwise, he would never have acted like that. They knowed it, so they couldn't be mad with him. The cancer was burrowing down deeper into him and hurting him more than it had the last three months it had been inside him. For the first time in them three months he had to take something for the pain, morphine, which put him in a comer and everything like that. They induced that comer 'cause he had become agitated something bad. Even combative was what Will told us. The respite people called in the family. Me and Bertie Mae and the younguns went up. Emory laid in that great big bed, not looking a bit like hisself, not a bit like the big old bear of a man he oncet was. Our brother. We used to call him Superman and Clark Kent, with his black hair and his black glasses and his big shoulders. But the kryptonite got him. The kryptonite called cancer. He just laid there in that bed with his eyes closed and his jaw hanging down slack and stiff like one of them ventriloquist dolls. Pitiful. More pitiful was how Emory's wife Doris sat beside his bed in her wheelchair just a-crying and squeezing Emory's hand over and over like she was trying to wake him up or something, and I reckon that's exactly what she was doing.

Two days later Emory was gone. Went out peaceful. In his sleep. Best way to go. We thanked the Good Lord for that. Wasn't like our daddy, Bert McMillan, who wasted away with his cancer, just shrunk and shrunk till one day he went away altogether.

When people in Compton die, they get buried by Rivers Funeral Home. White folks, I mean. The blacks has their own mortuary run by the Scott family. But for the whites it's the Rivers, who are so good at what they do, nobody else in the county even bothers trying to compete with 'em. The afternoon Emory passed we met at Rivers Funeral Home – me, Bertie Mae, Will McMillan, his sister Lisa, and poor old Doris in her wheelchair – to plan the ceremony. Pastor Olin from Mount of Glory Baptist, our home church, also showed up to pray and help with the plans. Will is a schoolteacher who teaches English, and him and Charlene Rivers come up with the words for the obituary that would run in the paper. And Lisa and Charlene talked about the music that would be played. And when we was done, we met over at Lisa's house to accept visitors. Folks from Mount of Glory and elsewhere was good enough to bring food – lots of it. Deli trays and Kentucky Fried Chicken and barbeque and cakes and pies and everything like that. Enough to eat on for a week. And we ate and talked and even laughed some as we remembered our brother and expressed thanks that he wasn't suffering no more and was in a better place and everything like that. He was better off than we was. That was for sure.

But Debbie Lynn couldn't let Emory be the center of things. Oh no ma'am. She had to have the attention for herself. Got in a corner of the living room off to herself with her phone in her lap and her lower lip poked out a mile. She hadn't up to then joined in on any of the remembering. Just sat there hoping somebody would feel sorry for her. Well, I don't know if I was sorry for her right then or not, but I went up to her and said, "What's the matter with you?"

She didn't look up from her phone when she told me," Lewis has done broke up with me again. Says he just wants to be friends and that's all."

Shit! (I wanted to say but did not, for the preacher from the Methodist church happened to be standing nearby, and while the Methodists ain't so strict as us Baptists, it is still not a good thing to cuss around a man of God.)

"You mean to tell me your uncle is laying a corpse over yonder at Rivers Brothers mortuary, and all you can do is sit here and mope over somebody who don't give two hoots about you? Ort to be ashamed."

She didn't say nothing back, so I went on.

"You ort to think about Emory and your mama and everybody else who's done suffered this loss. Get your mind off Lewis a while."

Well, it was like mashing a button, for not five minutes later, old Debbie Lynn perked up and set about taking control of the room.

"He loved me best!" she shouted out of nowhere, so's everybody turned to look at her. It was like some devil had got holt of her. Like in *The Exorcist*, you know, or some other scary movie. Her eyes was big and wide and they was this big, bright, scary smile on her face. She didn't really look at nobody else right then. Just stared off into someplace none of the rest of us could see. But she didn't stop talking, of course.

"Called me his 'Little Debbie Do.' He'd come back from somewheres and always bring me something back with him. A candy bar. A bracelet. It didn't matter. I was his "Little Debbie,' and he was my great big Bubba. Till *he* come along." And then she did look down at the rest of us and pointed right to Will McMillan, Emory's oldest child. Will just sat in his place and didn't seem to know what to think about being singled out and everything like that. Debbie had ambushed him. She went on.

"Sometimes I really hated you, Will McMillan, for taking my Bubba away from me. You come along, and there went my candy bars and my bracelets and my sweet kisses."

"He didn't give me any bracelets, Debbie Lynn, I promise you," Will finally said in defense of hisself. "But I sure did like those candy bars."

Everybody but Debbie Lynn laughed, right nervous-like.

Debbie Lynn went on that way for the longest and managed, oncet again, to wander away from Emory to everybody else, to every other man she had knowed in her life: her daddy that Bertie Mae divorced and that died hisself from the cancer, to Michael her dead son and Michael's no-count real daddy, to Jimmy Fulton, who treated her better than she deserved, and finally to Lewis Brown, that nasty old drunk who had only one use for Debbie Lynn, who was too dumb to see the fact.

Right then I thought to myself, "Damn, I got to be careful next time I ask for something, 'cause I just liable to get it again." I mean Debbie Lynn just wouldn't shut her mouth. Just went on and on telling the same thing over and over and laughing so loud at herself she left the living room ringing. She told about Lewis's dead wife and his daughter and how good a dancer Lewis was and everything like that, how good he was to her and he give her money and on and on. It distressed Bertie Mae, the way Debbie managed to change the subject to Lewis Brown and forget Emory. It got to everybody, I think, including me. We was tired of it. It took Debbie Lynn's younger sister Tina to end it. Tina just stood up, told everybody good night, and left. Pretty and clean as that. Wasn't too long after that everybody else followed her out the door, except the folks that lived there, of course, and for a minute I thought they might leave too, let Debbie Lynn have it all to herself.

Debbie Lynn left everybody with a bad feeling that night, going on like she done about old Lewis Brown, painting him out to be a saint when everybody knowed just the opposite was true. And it just got worser the next day, the day of Emory's funeral. It was one of the very worst things I have ever seen in my life.

First off, Debbie Lynn was late for the lunch the folks at Mount of Glory Baptist Church put on for the family in front of the service. She told Bertie Mae she would be late but not how come she would be late. Turns out, when she showed, she had been all the way to Gaffney that morning to see You Know Who, the old whoremonger hisself.

I said, "You mean to tell me you been up yonder with that old man all morning while your family is down here about to bury their brother, their daddy, their uncle? *Your* uncle?"

Debbie Lynn stepped back like I slapped her in the face.

She said, "We back together again. He called me last night so we could make up. Called. Not texted. And he ain't old. He ain't but sixty-eight."

"Old enough to know better."

"And look here." She stepped back some more and held out her arms.

"What is it?" I said.

"This dress." She had on a black skirt with a top that looked like it was made out of something you hang on Christmas trees. Right gaudy, I thought, especially for a funeral.

"What about that dress?"

"It belonged to Lewis's wife Peggy. He wanted me to wear it today. Had his daughter Theresa run fetch it for me in the bedroom closet."

"You got your own dresses," Bertie Mae said, standing nearby. "Why didn't you wear one of them?"

"Lewis wanted me to wear it. To show how much he cares for me and the whole family. I invited him to come down for the funeral, but he said no out of respect."

"Well, thank God for that."

Debbie Lynn's face got red at oncet. Her lips swelled up.

"I don't know what y'all got against him."

"He's a nasty old drunk that don't do nothing but use you, Debbie Lynn."

"He only gets drunk on the weekends. I done told y'all that a thousand times. During the week he's straight."

"Yeah. Sounds like a Sunday school teacher to me."

Tears lit up Debbie Lynn's eyes but didn't quite make it to falling.

"Nobody gives a damn whether I'm happy or not."

"Stop cussing in church."

"Nobody cares what I been through. How I buried a daddy, a granddaddy, a son, a husband. Now my uncle. My Bubba. The only one who ever did care." Then the tears fell, and Debbie Lynn looked like some old doll baby that's been left too long in the closet – her makeup messed up and everything like that. And she had dyed her hair blonde when she's been a brunette all her life. She done it 'cause that's what Lewis wanted. And I declare, the way she wore it long it looked like a wig or something. She just didn't have no dignity about her whatsoever.

"We all been through it, Debbie Lynn. Ever single one of us."

That's when she turned away from us and walked out of the big hall where we'd been having our lunch.

Her younger sister Tina come up in her place and said to me and Bertie Mae, "She shows herself today, and I will beat the hell out of her."

(Tina done that very thing to two of her ex-husbands before they become exes. Had one of 'em pinned up to the kitchen wall by his neck when the police showed up. So we knowed she was capable of hell-beating and everything like that.)

After lunch come the wake, and what was supposed to be a hour and a half visitation turned into nearly two hours. That's how well-knowed and well-liked our brother was. Everybody had worked with or for Emory at some point if they had worked at all in a cotton mill in Compton County, for Emory worked in pert-near all of them. And there was the Shriners and the Elks too, come to pay their respects and Daddy's and Mama's people from Compton and Gaffney and Spartanburg and everywhere else like that. You can't never say you have a good time at a funeral, but it was good to see kin and friends and other folks who had hid theirselves away some place for some time. We just talked and laughed and caught up and everything like that. And the folks at Rivers Brothers done a good job laying out Emory. He looked mostly like hisself 'cept his mouth might have been stretched some out of whack.

I kept a good eye on Miss Debbie Lynn to make sure she was behaving herself, and she was, mostly. Talked too much and too loud. But that ain't nothing unusual for her. I'm willing to bet the last dime I got in this world, she come out of Bertie Mae's cooter a-running her little pink mouth. She insisted on telling folks how she had got pretty much used to losing all the men in her life that she loved, how it was her what took care of her granddaddy, mine and Ruth's daddy, Bert McMillan, when he was dying of cancer – changing his diapers and everything like that. Which is a damned old nasty lie. She never did nothing for Daddy 'cept try to take as much of his Social Security check as she could every third of the month. I started to walk over yonder and slap her lying mouth. But I didn't. "Remember Emory," I told myself and took a deep breath. "Today's about your brother, not your lazy-ass lying niece."

When the wake was done, Preacher Olin led us into a room off the sanctuary. Johnny Dale Rivers, the head of Rivers Mortuary (now that his daddy and his daddy's brothers was gone) and the elected coroner of Compton, come with him. Pastor Olin prayed, and Johnny Dale give us instructions on how to proceed back into the sanctuary to begin the service and everything like that. Then we lined up at the sanctuary door. Pastor Olin offered up one more prayer. I looked over my shoulder with one eye open. Instead of praying with the rest of us, Debbie Lynn had her phone out and was texting. I hissed to all them behind me: "Tell her to put that thing up right now!" She heard me. She slipped it in the skirt of that old man's dead wife's dress, but she didn't look happy about doing it. Fact of business, she looked like she was about to break down and cry. I didn't know what that was about, and right then I could have cared less.

So we walked back in a line into the sanctuary, with everybody else, all the mourners and such, standing in the pews waiting for us, and we took our place and waited for Jim Waggoner, the assistant pastor, to say the opening prayer and to ask all of us to be seated. We did. There was Preacher Olin on the other side of the altar, not getting up from his seat right yet, because first there was to be a song from a young man that Bertie Mae's granddaughter Tiffany knowed. This young man stood in the choir loft, all by hisself, and with a tape recorder or some such playing behind him, he sang "How Great Thou Art," which Emory loved. It was his favorite gospel song, especially when Elvis Presley sang it. This boy had a good voice and done a good job. When he sat down, then Preacher Olin stood and begun his sermon. I like Preacher Olin and all. He's a good man, I think, and he's got a real nice family. But he ain't the most dynamite speaker in the pulpit you ever heard. He means well and all. But, I don't know, he just didn't give the audience a real clear picture of who Emory McMillan was. His sermon could have been about anybody really – Bob Smith or Joe Jones or Tom, Dick, or Harry. Maybe it's because he ain't from Compton or even South Carolina for that matter. Comes from someplace in Virginia, which is well and good. But I wished it would have been somebody close to Emory to give the eulogy. Like our cousin Jim Ed McMillan, who's been a preacher for years.

Anyway, Preacher Olin talked for a while then sat back down, and the singing boy got back up and sang "Just as I Am," which I did not know Emory cared for so much. (Would have been good if the boy had sung "Tennessee Waltz." That's Emory's most favorite song of them all, but I don't reckon that would have been appropriate for a funeral and everything like that.) The boy finished and took his seat. Preacher Olin got back up and spoke some more, quoting Bible verses and all. Then he turned to Jim Waggoner, who told us all to stand. The pall bearers also stood. Two of them was my boys, James, Jr., and Tom. As Jim led us in a chorus of "I'll Fly Away," the pallbearers went for Emory's casket and hoisted it up amongst theirselfs. As we was directed by Jimmy Dale Rivers, the family turned in the pews to leave, but first we had to wait for the pall bearers to take Emory's body up the aisle and to the church's front door.

And that's when it happened. When Debbie Lynn made her move.

She was setting on the outside end of one pew. Now and then during the service I'd look over at her. She had her head down mainly, her lips all stuck out, like she was more mad than sad, or God knows what. Otherwise, I didn't pay her no attention. Then we stood up at Jim Waggoner's orders. The casket come up the aisle. It got close to Debbie Lynn's pew. It met up with Debbie Lynn's pew. And Debbie Lynn, right on time, thowed up her arms and hollered out, "Oh no! Don't take him away! All the men I love is going away from me! My daddy, my papa, Michael, Jimmy, and my Bubba! Just take me along with them, Lord, 'cause I can't stand no more!" And with that, she fell – no, more like she give a little jump – on the casket so hard it went to the floor. She was heavy enough to take down with her not only the box with my brother in it but a couple of the pallbearers too. And for a second they laid there, the three of them, in a huddle, like they was playing football and trying to figure out the next play. The music stopped. Nobody didn't breathe a breath. I thought, "My God, I'm watching a movie or else dreaming whilst standing up on two feet in broad daylight. This can't be happening."

But it was.

Debbie Lynn done more than just fall and lay there. She kicked and flailed and hit out at anybody that tried to offer her a hand and went on about how nobody loved her no more and everything like that.

It was Bertie Mae's other daughter Tina that moved first in the middle of all that shock. She left the pew she was in and swooped down on Debbie Lynn like a hawk and hauled her up quick as lightning and had her out of that church almost before we knowed it. The pallbearers moved quick theirselfs once they got over what had just happened to them. They got hold of the casket. The music started back up. And the boys moved Emory's body in a dignified way like nothing ever happened.

Debbie Lynn did not make it to the graveside service. She stayed back in the car, which was just as well. God knows she might have got up and jumped in Emory's grave herself if she thought it might get her some attention. But we put Debbie Lynn out of our mind right then. What was important was remembering our good brother. And it was a good service too, especially when them boys from the United States Army played "Taps" on the trumpet and handed the United States flag to Emory's widow Doris. We all got a bit wet-eyed then. Even the boy playing the music cried, though he never missed a note.

Debbie Lynn done a bad, bad thing acting the way she done in the church, bringing all the attention to herself when it should all have been on Emory. It made for hard feelings for everybody. Bertie Mae wouldn't have nothing to do with Debbie Lynn for a long time, and her sister and niece wouldn't speak to her neither. Will McMillan and his sister Lisa acted all right to her, I reckon because they still needed her to come help stay with Doris till they found somebody else. I was mad with her too, but I still talked to her anyway. I reckon because I felt sorry for her. We found out that text she got right before the church service was from Lewis Brown, breaking up with her again. That's right. He sent her that news right before her uncle's funeral. That's the kind of lowdown, dirty-assed hound dog of an old goat he is, treating her that way when he knowed good and well she was in love with him and everything like that. And what's worse is Debbie Lynn ran up to Gaffney right after the funeral to go see him.

"I's just taking his wife's dress back," she told me later.

Shit!

She went up yonder to beg him to have her back is what she done. She acts like a teenage girl, when here she is nearly sixty years old. She's an old dog herself. And you know what they say about old dogs and new tricks.

They don't rightly get along with each other.

Mr. Aldon

When my father died, Aldon Keane attended his wake in soiled jeans and a stained tee-shirt, his face a mask of tears. He did not drift in or approach us with quiet dignity. He hurtled into the sanctuary as though trying to forestall an emergency, to ward off the cancer that had killed Daddy. He did not have the limp that once identified his walk. He moved smoothly and was met halfway down the aisle by the funeral director, Bradley Rivers.

"He's pitiful," my sister commented beside me, her hand on my elbow. "He's lost without Daddy. Bless it."

"He's got to make a show of things," I replied. "It's just like him."

Lisa, my sister, squeezed my arm in gentle reprimand then went over to give Avery a proper greeting as representative of the McMillan family. My mother, in a wheelchair, incapacitated by a stroke and attendant maladies, could not fulfill the functions that would normally have gone to the deceased's wife. Or to his son.

The visitation, an open coffin affair, was held at Mount of Glory Baptist Church, the family place of worship for more than sixty years. I remained at the first center pew among other mourners watching as Lisa embraced Aldon and patted his back. They talked for several minutes; I wondered what about and decided, knowing Aldon as I did, that he was exacting from Lisa a promise, as if she were in a position to make it and keep it, that he could go on doing the jobs he had been doing for Daddy the last few years – cutting grass, clearing the yard of debris, washing cars, etc. – for which Daddy paid him, depending on the task, anywhere from twenty-five to sixty dollars. Aldon's tears were not crocodilian; they were genuine. He wept, I was convinced, at the prospect of loss of income.

I didn't like him or trust him and never had. This mistrust went all the way back to the day he walked into my university classroom some five or six years earlier. He was unkempt and non-traditional, maybe thirty-five, thin, with facial hair and the aforementioned limp. His shirt-tails were out and his pupils were starkly red. He smiled at me without a word and took a seat at the back of the class. His name was not on my official roll. When the period was over he came up to my desk to explain.

"My check ain't come yet, sir. So I can't pay the tuition right now. When it come I can pay. Mr. Tony in the office say I got a week to pay it."

I was skeptical. Then he winced.

"You all right?"

"No sir. It's my legs. I got the old man legs. They bother me something awful. It's 'cause I got to walk everywhere I go, Mr. McMillan. All over Compton County. Ain't got the money for a car. Not yet. But I'm working on it." He winced again, even more profoundly than at first. "Oh ain't no good going to come from this!" When he had recovered from the pain, he looked back down at me as I sat at my desk. "I want this so bad, Mr. McMillan. This education. All I done my whole life is work a hard, mean, ugly job. One after the other. Stooping and lifting. In the heat of the sun. Ninety degrees usually or more. Or the freezing cold. Take your pick. It's all hateful. I don't want to go on like that and die before my time. You know?"

I told him I sympathized with him and wished him good luck, but it was a hollow sentiment, meant merely to expedite his departure from my classroom. Right away, as soon as he limped into my class, he gave off the scent of being a fake, a charlatan, a huckster, and I really had no idea why. It was all intuition. He seemed too good to be true – or too bad to be true, in his own melodramatic case. He went on a little while longer, observing that people in Compton could no longer count on a good, steady textile job, that almost all the mills had moved to Mexico. He wasn't telling me anything I didn't already know; my father had spent practically all his long working life in textiles. Then he held out his hand to me and shuffled off to the door, crouching and wincing before he exited, moaning, "Oh these old man legs! Ain't nothing good coming from this!"

A few minutes later I found the school's chief admissions officer, Tony Buchanan, at his desk.

"Don't worry about it," Tony told me. "He doesn't have all his paperwork filled out, and he can't pay tuition. I'm not even sure he has his GED. Not sure why he showed up in the first place. He knows better. If he shows again, just let me know, and I'll take care of it."

And he did. Aldon. Show. The next class. And the next few classes. No matter how I hinted, he kept coming. For some reason I didn't want to come right out and say, "Stop coming to my class!" I abhorred confrontation and always had, and certainly I didn't want things to blow up in front of other students. That's an unnecessary ugliness. Scenes are not my scene. Drama should remain on the stage. So Aldon continued sitting in the back, grinning at me and nodding, as though every academic point I enunciated made perfect sense to him. (And who knows? Perhaps it did. At least he was listening, unlike so many of the traditional students, too engaged with their gadgets to give a damn.) I emailed Tony Buchanan, and Aldon soon disappeared from my class and from campus itself. The problem had been solved, or so I thought.

Six months later I was driving to my parents' after concluding office hours that day. Pauline, my wife, was out of town at a conference for secondary ed teachers in Raleigh, North Carolina. I'd been invited home for supper, a pleasure I never turned down if I could help it. As I neared their property I noticed a small, slumped figure in the front yard, cutting the grass, yanking the mower back and forth almost rhythmically. My throat went a bit dry. I thought I knew who it was. And it was confirmed when I pulled into the driveway. It was Aldon Keane in jeans and a sleeveless denim shirt, his face and small dark muscles slick with sweat. He noticed me over the noise of his work. His wet face grew a smile. He stopped the mower and waited for me to exit my car. I did, slowly, not wanting to confront him, but it was inevitable. He came to me with his right hand out.

"Mr. Will! Mr. Will! How you doing today, young man? My, what a good-looking car you got! Hope to have one myself not too long from now."

I took his hand reluctantly and said, "I had no idea you were a yardman," which wasn't exactly true. He had, after all, related the hardships of his profession that first day in class.

"Oh yes. Been one since I was ten years old. I've always worked outdoors. How are things at the college, Mr. Will?"

"Educational," I replied, not really meaning to be nasty but unable to help it.

He laughed a bit as though he appreciated the humor then said, "I plan to get back up there one day."

I went on into the house. Mama and Daddy were setting the last of the supper things on the kitchen table.

"Where in the world did you find Aldon Keane?" I asked Daddy at once, in place of a greeting.

"He found *me*," Daddy said. "He's been cutting Mr. Davis's grass across the road for a long time. Finished one afternoon and came down here and asked me if I'd like him to cut mine. I said yes."

"He does that. Just appears and presumes."

"You know him?"

I explained.

"I tell you what though, Will. He's a worker. Does a good and thorough job."

"What you paying him?"

Mr. Aldon

He told me.

"Be careful. I don't fully trust him."

"How come?"

"I don't know."

"That's a good reason. That's a hell of a reason."

Mid-way through our meal a knock came at the back door, mere feet from the table. No one said "Come in," but the door opened anyway, and there stood Aldon Keane, flesh a-glitter with sweat.

"Mr. Emory!" he hollered as though at a football stadium and Daddy were sitting a mile away.

"Aldon!" Daddy responded and stood.

"Got your grass cut, sir. All done."

"Good man, good man," Daddy said and moved so as to push Aldon back outdoors, to pay him, I presumed.

When Daddy came back in, I said, "It's a wonder Aldon didn't invite himself to supper."

"I invited him," Daddy said, resuming his chair at the table. "He said no thanks. Maybe next time." After a while he asked, "You don't like him?"

"I don't know. He insinuates himself in a disagreeable way. He's pushy. I don't like pushy people."

"I tell you what though: He's a worker."

He continued to service my folks' lawn up to the time of my father's last illness, when fall arrived and the grass was not so persistent or prolific. Then we did not see him again until the funeral. Up to then he did what was, admittedly, a good and thorough job. He *was* a good worker. To deny that fact would be total dishonesty. But he was a suspicious character as well. I worried he might go into the house and take something or try to persuade my father to pay him more than the job actually deserved. These suspicions were not at all compelled by race. Aldon could have been any race and I would have doubted his sincere intentions. It was his overenthusiastic way of greeting a person, as though he had known him or her forever. It was all that Mister business – Mister Emory, Mister Will, Mister Mister. It all had a TV preacher unctuousness to it, or worse, so that one could almost see the grease stains in the air when Aldon departed.

Once I went home unexpectedly, uninvited, and there sat Aldon at the supper table with Mama and Daddy, at the place I sat when I ate there, the remains of one of Mama's succulent baked roasts on his plate.

"Mr. Will! Mr. Will!" he shouted upon seeing me and stood up. "Come on in here, young man, and get you some of this good home cooking!"

"You should have told us you were stopping by," Daddy said. "We would have had a plate set for you already."

Aldon excused himself and left. He had finished his job and, I assumed, been paid for it in money and meat. "Thank you, Mr. Emory! Thank you, Miss Doris!" he called on his way out. "It sure was delicious, ma'am."

I took the chair he had sat in and filled my own plate with roast and carrots and potatoes, which I then picked at glumly.

"That Aldon's a character, ain't he?" Daddy said with a short laugh.

"I guess he pushed his way in here," I replied. "Wormed his way in as usual."

"You just don't like him, do you?"

I didn't say anything.

Mr. Aldon

"Ah, he's all right. A mite forward, but he's just a poor old crippled-up young man looking to make a dollar here and there. He's not the only one. And he's a durn good worker too."

A half hour later I left Mama and Daddy and was surprised and startled to find Aldon still in the yard, leaning on Daddy's 2002 Ford Taurus as though it were his, smoking. He saw me, grinned, tossed down the cigarette, and rubbed it into the ground with his shoe. This was the ground he had not long ago "tended." I fished for the car key in my trousers.

"You know what, Mr. Will?" he said as I neared my car, also a Taurus. "I believe you got the best daddy there is."

"I think you're right, Aldon. Thank you."

"He give a man a chance when lots other folks can't be bothered. You know? He give me one right here. This work in his yard. And I've heard about how he was in the mills from the folks who worked for him. The way he helped 'em out. Going out in his own car to pick 'em up and take 'em to work when there was snow or ice on the ground and they didn't have no other way. Passing 'em a little bit of his own cash if they come up short on pay day and need to pay the light bill before the lights gets turned off. He got a crown in heaven waiting on him. I'm sure of it!"

I smiled in the growing twilight and turned to unlock the car door. He caught my arm, which made me turn back to him.

"You know what, Mr. Will? Me and you's two different men trying to do the best we can with what we know how to do best. You with your books, me with my hands. Ain't one of us better nor worser than the other. We just different."

"I never said otherwise."

He smiled and let go of my arm. "My dear, precious old dead grandma used to say, 'Everything chicken but the bone. Cut it up, cook it right, be chicken right on.' And she had a little variation to it too, Mr. Will. Said, 'Everything chicken but the bill. Cut it up, cook it right, be chicken still.' What she meant was it's all good. It's all life, living no matter how you cut it up. You at the college, me in the yard. It's all the same when it's thowed in the pot to be cooked."

I smiled at him and got into my automobile.

At Mount of Glory Baptist during my father's wake, he took my arm again. I thought he'd left the church, gone on back outdoors, but no. I turned and saw him still crying.

"Mr. Will," he said, voice choked. "What we gone do without him, Mr. Will? What we gone do without Mr. Emory?" He forced himself upon me. He gripped me in his long muscular arms. His face wet my shoulder. Other people were watching. I know I should have returned the embrace, even if for appearance's sake only. But I couldn't. I just couldn't do it.

A Death By The River

The woman and her mother had idled away the afternoon together, anesthetized by the drone of the old fashioned television set in front of them, broad and heavy as a walnut cabinet. Game shows, talk shows, doctor shows – all had found at least temporary display there in the small clapboard house by the Selden River. Judge Judy though was ruled intolerable ("Too hateful," daughter and mother agreed), and at last they settled upon an early evening news broadcast. And just in time too.

The scrubbed, clean, and shining face of a Spartanburg news anchor appeared, and beneath her vociferously animated mouth a blue band stretched with the announcement: COMPTON COUNTY MAN MURDERED, leaving a fresh wound in Judy Jarman's breast.

"Lookee yonder!" Mrs. Winstead cried. "There it is! They talking about it right now." Judy had given her mother the remote control for her own pacification. Anything to keep her there with her. She had needed her company so much that morning, that she had driven over to pick up Mrs. Winstead from her own home, and Mrs. Winstead lived only a block over. It was the noise that had gotten to Judy – the sirens, the sounds of voices, an unknown, unseen source of hurrying past her house that never would seem to quit, the stamping of feet, the hollering, "Did ya hear? Did ya hear?" And then she had turned on the radio station to WBFC and found out the reason for the commotion, and she had nearly gone to her knees in distress and disbelief. She had thought of burrowing back into her bed, covering herself with quilts, and try to dig herself to someplace where such news did not exist.

Mrs. Winstead proceeded to raise the volume even higher, so that the anchor's professional, accent-free voice deafened everything else in the house.

"Mama," Judy said impatiently, but she could not help watching the story, listening again to the details of Bobby K. Thompson's murder.

Bobby K. Thompson. Fifty-four years old. Former textile worker. Former mechanic. Lived alone in his own house in Selden, the river town in southeastern Compton County, ten minutes from the county seat itself. Retired from employment following a stroke that left him partially paralyzed. Never married. No children. Found dead that morning by his brother Cedric Thompson after Mr. Thompson's repeated failed attempts to reach his brother by telephone. Cause of death: blunt force trauma to head and neck. Petty larceny also discovered: Robert K. Thompson's wallet discarded empty beside him, personal documents scattered about. A pair of Walther pistols also gone. And some family jewelry. Heirlooms. Robert K. Thompson lived with his mother Althea until she died. Her wedding ring gone, along with other valuables. A vile, racist message spray-painted crudely on one side of the clapboard house: (The television camera avoided the offending word, leaving viewers to guess what it was.) Cedric Thompson facing the camera, bearded and gray, eyes brimming, head shaking, voice chanting: "Why, why, why? He was a good boy. Why?"

That's right, Judy thought in her own present inarticulateness, so loudly she thought her mother might have heard it. A good boy. "One of the good ones," her daddy had said. Meaning the coloreds. "They ain't all good like him. But when you get a good one, why, you done found the best person on the face of the earth." Bobby was always helpful. It didn't matter how tired out he might be from a long day or night at Compton Mill or at the garage where he helped to rebuild motors: if Mr. Winstead needed him, Bobby would be there, whether it was mowing the lawn or repairing a shingle on the roof or some other chore menial or major. *He would be there.* It was almost as though he had a sixth sense for Mr. Haskell's (that's what Bobby called Judy's daddy) needed. Sometimes he would show up at the Winsteads' doorstep unbidden, smiling widely when the door opened upon him, and inquiring, "Mr. Haskell got anything for me to do today? If so, I'm ready and raring to do it!" His appearance at their doorstep became even more frequent after Mr. Winstead's own stroke. He was a Godsend. That's what Judy's mother called him, and she had no qualms about inviting him in to supper or about making supper for him to send home for him and his mother.

As for Judy, she didn't know what to make of him. She had grown up with black men and gone to school with them, of course, and sat in restaurants and movie theaters with them. It was the nineteen seventies after all when she grew up. But Bobby K. Thompson wasn't like any other person she knew, black or white. "A good boy," her daddy had called him without the least racial taint to the word. But boys weren't good, no matter their color. They were loud and mean and selfish. They picked their noses and dug into their crotches and swore and fought at the least provocation. And if they didn't swear or fight, if they were passive, why what account were they? None she could think of. Better to be mean and nasty than to show no joy in living whatsoever.

Bobby K. Thompson was neither mean nor nasty, but he was no wallflower either. He laughed a lot good-naturedly and had bright eyes that promised harmless mischief and strong hands made that way from so much hard work so early on in his life. Judy Winstead was six years younger than Bobby K. Thompson, so they had no chance to go to school together, but she had heard from others how popular he was, how on the almost newly integrated Selden High School grounds he moved easily among the population, the whites, the blacks, seamlessly, accepted by all, appreciated for his humor and optimism and strong handshake or backclap. Those few times early on when Judy had caught glimpses of Bobby in Selden, she held him in awe, remembering all the good things she had heard about him. How could one man contain so much goodness? He was like Jesus in a way, bringing people together, knowing no strangers, dispensing so much kindness. Surely there was no one else like him, at least not in Selden. Probably not even in South Carolina.

Then she had her chance to know him better. His father died, and for whatever reason, his mother had decided to move the family closer to the river, to a home not too far from the Winsteads. There were some rumblings in the community about the appearance of blacks but not many. The Thompsons were quiet and kept to themselves. And it wasn't long after that, Bobby and Judy made their first "introduction" to each other. It occurred in summer, a day whose stifling heat promised rain and maybe something worse. Judy had decided to run away from home. She was ten years old then, a big girl, too big to be told what to do all the time by her mama and daddy. So she fixed up a knapsack with everything she thought she needed and headed up the road towards Compton. Her ultimate destination: Myrtle Beach, where she could live on the beach if she wanted and be her own woman. She had had no idea she was marching off in the wrong direction, east instead of west.

She had left the Selden town limits and gotten onto the main highway, where each side of the road dropped away to long, deep gullies choked with kudzu and guarded over by very still pine trees. Then, suddenly, like the exhalation of a giant's breath, a wind ran over the trees, bending them, ruffling the grass like showgirls' skirts. Clouds quickened. The sky turned skillet black then bell-pepper green. Judy had never witnessed anything like it nor been more scared. She stopped in the middle of the road. There was no one else there and nowhere to go: desolation waited on either side of the highway. Lightning flashed. Then she felt the first large drops of rain, dense and cold as ice cubes. She panicked and turned back towards Selden and ran, dropping her knapsack. The cold rain did not suppress the July heat. Judy ran with rain and sweat stinging her eyes. She closed her eyes, which she shouldn't have; she could no longer see where she put her feet and tripped over an indiscriminate clod of dirt and fell. She rolled half-way down the gully and lay there letting the hail pummel her. She thought: "Mama has told God to find me and punish me for running away, and He's done it. He's done it!" She might as well just lie there and endure her punishment. You couldn't outrun God.

She didn't see the red pickup truck pulling to the side of the road, nor hear the young black man leaving it to come after her. But she did feel his arms lifting her and carrying her off. She did hear him say repeatedly, "It's all right, sweet thing. It's all right." He used a blanket in the truck to dry her off, but she had been scared beyond reason. She even fought him some, but he held her wet and trembling to him and rocked her as he would have a child much younger. He sang to her: "My Lord Hath Made the Promise." She calmed down, suddenly pacified by the heat of his body and the warm sonority of his singing voice. In fact, she went off to sleep right there in the front seat of his truck, overcome by fear and fatigue. The next thing she remembered was waking up in her own bed with her mother looking down at her and feeding a thermometer carefully into her mouth.

And later, but not much so, came the time, in fall, when Bobby K. Thompson, now the Winsteads' neighbor, offered to clean their gutters of leaves. The ladder was propped against the house. Bobby worked away. Judy stood below and watched him. By then she had come to regard him with something that approached the mystical. He was, after all, her hero. And standing there in the brittle autumn grass, watching him fling down handfuls of leaves like the carcasses of old fish, she wondered if he would do it again – save her. What if she jumped into the Selden River and didn't know how to swim? Would he come after her again? What if the house was burning up? Or a stranger dragged her off with ugly intent? Would he come for her? An idea occurred to her. She knew that ladder was old and rickety. It might have been older than her mama and daddy. One good stamp and it would break to pieces. She went to it and began to climb it till she reached half-way. That was when she hollered at Bobby K. Thompson: "You need help up yonder?"

Bobby K. turned from his work. "No ma'am. And you get down from there. Mr. Haskell would skin me and you both if he seen you on that ladder."

"No he won't."

"Get down from there please, Judy."

"No! I'm staying right here." And to accent her defiance she bounced on the rung which held her. She heard it pop and crack. It gave way finally, and she had gone sailing backwards through the warm smoky air until she landed on the ground with a thud. She cried out in pain that was not entirely make believe. Bobby K. heard her and came down the broken ladder with the speed of a silent movie character in jeopardy. He took her up in his arms, the same as he had done a few months earlier in the July hailstorm.

"You all right? You all right?" he repeated.

She opened her eyes and nodded. Then she smiled.

"I don't see what's to smile about," he replied but did not let her loose. "It looks like I'm going to have to follow you around everywhere you go, Judy Winstead, just to make sure you don't kill yourself."

She smiled again and said drowsily, "That's all right with me."

Whether or not she was in love with Bobby K. Thompson, she could not say for sure. She loved him. She knew that. But whether or not there was any carnal or romantic element contained in that love was unclear to her. In a way she hoped not. Only white trash "went" with black people. Judy had heard that her whole growing up life. It was an unwritten Compton rule. And the women who went with black men back then were often pitied or scorned, never admired, never encouraged. "Oh that's the best she can do, ugly as she is," someone inevitably remarked when such an unfortunate creature happened by in public or became the subject of conversation. Judy didn't want to end up the target of such talk, so of course she never spoke of her feelings to anyone. But at night, away from the scornful, gossiping, hateful world, she found herself recalling with pleasure the warmth of Bobby K. Thompson's voice, the comfort of his eyes, the strength of his touch. Such pleasant, secret thoughts were a delicious kind of conspiracy against everyone else around her.

But when Bobby K. graduated from high school, he headed straight for the military, the U.S. Army, and was gone from South Carolina for six years. That gave Judy herself time to graduate, to meet Don Ray Jarman, to marry Don Ray Jarman, and to miscarry twice. By the time Bobby returned to South Carolina and took a job at Compton Mill in the spinning room, Judy had given birth to a son and later a daughter. By the time Bobby had quit the mill and gone to work for a local garage, Judy had lost her daddy, Mr. Haskell and divorced Don Ray because of his infidelity. And by the time Cedric Thompson had found his brother's body in their mother's house near the Selden River, any affection for Bobby, either illicit or pure, had been long buried in the deep folds of Judy Jarman's memory.

Presently, Judy's mother said, "I'm satisfied Jesse Jackson and that bunch will be down here to protest. He loves a TV camera like a hog loves slop. Of course if it had been a white man they'd found dead up yonder, old Jesse wouldn't bother rousing hisself."

"I reckon, Mama," Judy replied, still feeling some acute discomfort. Oh, some things belonged buried! So why didn't they stay that way?

At once the two women heard some noise and movement to their right, the sounds of slight commotion. This came from Judy's daughter Heather's bedroom. Heather had been there all day, mostly sleeping, and had not gotten up even for any dinner. A radio alarm clock blared out a current Top Forty music hit. But the song was drowned out by the sounds of Heather banging the clock silent with her fist and shouting, "Damnit!"

Shortly afterward, the bedroom door opened, and there Heather stood. She hadn't even bothered changing out of the tee-shirt and blue jeans she had worn the day before.

"Lord, girlie," Mrs. Winstead began. "How come you bothering to get up now? It's nearly bed time. Ought to just stay in the bed."

Heather was a tall, lean girl whose leanness nevertheless gave off an indication of muscularity and made for an intimidating figure. She wrinkled her nose at her grandmother's observation but otherwise ignored it. She traipsed from her bedroom to the bathroom behind Mrs. Winstead, not even bothering to excuse herself as she momentarily blotted out the television screen from her mother's and grandmother's view.

When the bathroom door shut, Mrs. Winstead turned to Judy and said, "And how old is the girl? Twenty-two, twenty-three years old? Old enough to act better than what she does. You ought to make her go get a job or put her out on her tailbone for good. That's what I'd do."

"I know, Mama," Judy said quietly and thought about how much Heather was like her daddy, Don Ray Jarman. Mean and shiftless, the both of them. She even looked like him, had that tough, lean muscular structure to her that her daddy had, the kind that belies hidden strength and viciousness, as well as the long, homely nose and chin. By all rights, Heather should have been living with her daddy, but then again, the two of them, Heather and Don Ray, would have starved to death, lazy as they were. And where was Don Ray these days anyway? Judy didn't keep up with him, and neither did their children. (Even Heather berated him in public each chance she got.) Judy wasn't sure he was even still living in Compton County. The last she had heard, he was shacked up with some gal twenty years his junior, and the girlfriend was the one working and paying all the bills. Judy knew all about that. She had done it herself for years. That was one reason she had left Don Ray. Frankly, she didn't care where he was or what had happened to him.

In a way, with Heather being there, it was almost as though Don Ray had never left. She was just like her daddy, except more of him, meaning she was lazier and meaner, so much so that Judy sometimes found herself wondering if the girl didn't scare her a little bit. It was not only the squinted look of her eyes which she always used to look at anybody; it wasn't just her physical threat or the fact she wasn't pretty. She had done things, or at least Judy thought she had, that put her mother to wondering. Like the time she nearly caught the house on fire playing with matches, striking one after another with no purpose other than to watch them flame out and give off that odor peculiar to burnt matches. She dropped one – Judy saw her – deliberately, still aflame, and watched as it caught the end of a newspaper that had been folded and discarded on the floor. The flame rose. Heather sat and watched it, smiling. It was Judy who had to put it out, stamping it repeatedly with her foot. There was the cruelty to animals and always the smart mouth, the talking back, the ugly remarks that came always as threats, even when they weren't, expressed in the direct gruffness a young woman like Heather might use to make threats. And she didn't work and seemed to have no inclination for such. She took it for granted that Judy would keep her up from now until always, without consulting Judy in the matter and with no display of gratitude, either verbal or physical. At times Judy felt she had the strength to run her off, but inevitably she backed down at the crucial moment of ejection. *No, no,* a warning voice told her. *What will she do if....*

The bathroom door opened. Heather stood in it, tall enough to touch the ceiling with her forehead if she wished to.

"You ought to have stayed in yonder and got you a bath. You stink."

After a moment Heather replied, "Who asked you, old lady?"

Mrs. Winstead drew back in her seat. "Didn't nobody ask me. Didn't nobody have to. I'm old. I'll say what I please when I please." She drew in her mouth and sniffed at her granddaughter. "What did you do all night? Paint? You smell like a paint brush."

Judy thought she had detected the same odor when Heather passed by her.

"Of course painting is work, and you ain't about to go nowhere near that, are you?"

Acrylic paint. Judy quickly convinced herself that was the smell coming from her daughter.

"What were you doing last night, Heather? And was there some reason you didn't call me to let me know where you were?"

"Yeah, the reason is I'm old enough to where I don't have to call nobody and tell them anything. And if you must know, I was out with friends."

"Friends? What friends? And all night? What did you do with your friends all night?"

"It was Travis and Blake. And we hung out. That's all. What do you think we did? Have a threesome or something?" Heather cackled. "We hung out and talked about how much we can't stand this goddamned stink hole of a town."

"That's nice," Mrs. Winstead remarked ironically. "Taking the Lord's name in vain. You going to stand for that, Judy? You sure wasn't raised by me to stand for it." Mrs. Winstead continued to inspect her granddaughter, hoping very much to come upon something else she might be able to criticize. She found it.

"And you ought to change clothes, child. What's that on your shirt? You cut yourself? Is that blood on your shirt? What is it, girlie?"

Heather yanked away the shirt hem Mrs. Winstead had caught hold of. "None of your damn business." Judy, watching the two of them, swallowed dryly. She regarded her daughter exclusively – this frame of external and internal ugliness – and wondered with grief if she had really given birth to such a monster. The fact had caused her to swoon in her seat and nearly pass out. Thank God there have been better days in my life, she thought so vehemently she nearly expressed the idea out loud. *Days before....*

"Where were you, Heather? Who were you with? What did you do?"

"I done told you, Mama. Now be quiet! I'm trying to watch the TV."

The news of Bobby K. Thompson's apparent murder still occupied the local broadcast. The young black woman reporting from Selden itself, just a couple of blocks away, reiterated the finer points of the case and interviewed the Compton County sheriff, who told her that as of yet, no leads in the crime had come open but would eventually. The whole community was outraged, he went on, and it might very well be Compton citizens rather than law enforcement who apprehended the suspect or suspects. Behind them stood gawking onlookers, people Judy thought she recognized, although many of them were young. Then she watched Heather watching and noticed with near-sickness the gleam that came into her daughter's small, hard eyes, the smile that threatened to open her small, hard mouth into a sneer.

"That bitch thinks she knows everything, don't she?" she commented eventually. "Listen to her. Coming down here and sticking her nose where it don't belong. They say she's been down here all day bothering people."

"How would you know that, Heather? You been in bed all day. How would you know what's going on?"

"I been in bed, but I ain't been asleep the whole time, Mama. Jesus Christ, you sure are dense sometimes. I know what's going on. Don't you worry." As though she had sensed that Judy was worried. Heather continued to stare at the screen, and her hatred for the reporter was a palpable thing in the room; it nearly drew two visible laser beams of malice towards the TV. "They think they can do anything now. Especially since that thing got to be President. Oh they're all over the place now. Can't turn on the TV without seeing one."

Judy had several turns of mind, none of them reassuring to her. But one stuck with her and dug at her, even though she fought it, pushed it away from her as too ridiculous even to consider.

What if my daughter, my flesh and blood...

"They're taking over."

Was capable of...

"You'd think they was the majority rather than the minority. What are they, ten million? Fifteen?"

Of...that?

"I don't know, Heather. I ain't had time to study on it. But, girlie, you better get one thing straight. Whether you like it or not, they's going to be black people in Heaven. As long as they accept Jesus Christ as their Savior, they got as much right to be there as me or you."

Murder!

"Yeah, they'll be there – as long as there's housing projects and handouts."

Judy became nauseated by fear and speculation. She chewed on the back of her hand but barely felt the pain she caused herself.

"Well, so what if another one's dead? Who'll miss him? Good riddance, I say."

"You just shut your mouth right now!"

Both Heather Jarman and Mrs. Winstead looked to their mother and daughter and found, with shock, that Judy had risen so quickly from her seat the neither of them had heard her. She stood, ashen-faced and trembling, pointing at her daughter. "Just shut your filthy mouth! "she repeated, and the imperative nearly toppled her over with its strength and vehemence.

"Judy, you all right?"

"Mama, you had a stroke or something? You want me to call 911?"

"I want you to quit talking about somebody you didn't even know. And you didn't know him. And wishing him dead like that." She sobbed and ran a hand over her face to clear the new tears. "Ain't you got a bit of soul in you, Heather? A bit of what makes somebody a human being?" She lowered her hand a moment before renewed potency possessed her. "I'll tell you what: they's heaps of folks before

Bobby K. Thompson that need to be dead. Lots of 'em! Pure wastes of flesh and blood is what they are, but they go on living. And for what? I couldn't tell you. God only knows. To add more misery to the world, I reckon. Fifty-four. That's how old he was, and some no good animal took him away. Beat him like a hog, and in his own house! Oh, you wouldn't have found a better human being on the face of the earth than Bobby K. Thompson, black or white? Would you, Mama?"

Mrs. Winstead said nothing.

"Nobody kinder or gentler or more willing to help his fellow man. He was the best person I knew outside my own mama and daddy. Certainly a lot better than that useless daddy of yours."

"Well you should have married him then," Heather shouted across the room.

"You're right. I should have. Because I loved him. That's right. Loved him! *I was in love with Bobby Thompson*. And I don't care what anybody has to say about it."

Heather's already plain face assumed a sinister scowl. "I could throw up, hearing you talk like that. You make me sick."

"Did you do it?" Judy asked abruptly, not entirely meaning to.

"Did I do what?"

"Did you...?" but she couldn't finish.

"What?" Heather heaved forth, taking a couple of steps towards her mother.

"Kill him?" Judy finished. "Are you and your friends the ones that did those things to him and left him for dead? I don't want to think it, Heather, but....the way you talk and smell and...."

Heather shook her head slowly. "You have done gone and lost your mind. *You're crazy!*"

Judy put both her hands to her face and cried into them. She shook with her sobs. Heather took the opportunity of this pause to cross the floor. When she neared Judy, Judy grabbed her by the arm. "I don't want to think it, Heather!" Heather shook off her mother's hand and returned to her room. She slammed the bedroom door behind her so hard, it shook the entirety of the small house.

"Judy," her mother called quietly. Meanwhile the television news played on at its same high volume.

Judy shook her head, still crying so hard she thought she would never stop. She sat back down. Her mother waited a few moments before saying, "You got to be careful what you say, Judy. You just hurt is all 'cause you lost a friend. You liable to think anything right now. You can't go and say just anything, no matter how bad it hurts." When Judy did not respond but kept her place and continued to cry, Mrs. Winstead finally stood up and carefully left the den for the guest room. Shortly afterwards Judy felt all cried out. She let her hands drift to her lap and looked up to see that the six o'clock news had now replaced its five o'clock equivalent, but the broadcast was occupied by the same story that had concerned it all through the day: the murder of Bobby K. Thompson in Selden, South Carolina. The young black woman reporter recounted all the previous details; there were no new ones apparently, no breaks in the case so far. She reported all this just a couple of blocks up from where Judy Jarman sat. A van engine roared behind her. The cameraman's bright white light illuminated her harshly.

Then Judy had an idea. She would get up and go out, dressed just as she was, and walk the two blocks and find this young woman and tell her *everything* – about Bobby Thompson and how she felt about him and how he was, aside from her daddy, of course, the best man she had ever known. She didn't care what Heather or her mother or anybody else thought. She would do it. She would make sure the whole, true story of a good man got told.

The Dead Will Provide

There could not have been anybody else in all of Beaslap, South Carolina, who loved a dead body more than Miss Semona Diggs.

Or at least a wake.

I don't say such a thing to be gross or nasty. It's just a fact. It has to be! Because who else in all our little place attended the wake of each and every corpse that got laid out to be looked at? (Until she herself became a corpse, that is.)

Nobody else I know.

And I hear she used to go all the way into Compton sometimes too if she found out about the passing of a black man or woman or child, just to be part of the public grieving.

When I said something about this to my mama, Mama said, "I wouldn't worry about it none, Jasmine. Seems to me like a right Christian thing to do."

Nah. Mama knew better. But it wasn't the time to argue right then.

She knew, and everybody else knew too, that Semona Diggs went to these showings of the dead for one reason and one reason only: for the eats.

The food people brought.

I don't know about anyplace else, because I've only lived here, in Beaslap, and I don't know if it is true of all or many white people in Compton County, but when a black person dies in Beaslap, Lord, here come their relations loaded down with enough food to fill a general store. But it's not store-bought, not any of it, except maybe the loaf bread and the soda pop. It's homemade and there's enough to feed an army for a week or more.

Fried chicken.

Baked chicken.

Ham and pork chops.

Barbecued ribs.

Green beans and collards.

Potato salad.

Corn creamed and steamed and still on the cob.

Okra.

Sweet taters.

Baked taters.

Cole slaw.

Goat hash and deer hash.

Macaroni and cheese.

Pasta salad.

Biscuits.

Rolls.

Loaf bread.

Cakes:

chocolate

red velvet

carrot

Pies:

pecan

sweet tater

apple and cherry.

And tea. Rivers and oceans of tea caught in plastic jugs. Soda too. And water and diet soda too for all the ones that's got high blood sugar.

It's like a party instead of a funeral, and I guess really that's what it is and should be. We're celebrating the person leaving this life and going on to meet his Savior in a place where there is no more sickness and suffering.

"Mama," I said when it was the right time to argue – or at least I thought – "Semona Diggs goes to see dead folks just so she can eat their food. And that's the only reason she goes."

Mama waited a minute before she answered. Then she said, "You don't know that." And that was all for the moment.

For some reason I was hot on the topic that day. "She don't know most of the people she goes to see. Nor their families. My goodness, the woman's as close as you can get to a hermit. Stays shut up in her house most of the time down on Cleaver Street. And she don't want anybody around her either. You step on her property, and she comes flying out the house like a wet hen just squawking for you to leave. But now when somebody drops dead, oh she's the first one to show up."

"So?"

"She never brings a dish herself."

"Maybe this is the way the Lord provides for Miss Diggs. Gives her the company she don't ordinarily have."

"She don't want company. She wants a drumstick and thigh with a side of tater salad. Ought to go to KFC for that and leave dead folks alone."

"Oh Jasmine."

It's true.

There was that time Mr. Ernest Freeman passed on the Dearborn Road in Beaslap. Good man. Everybody liked him. He cut hair and built houses and drove a taxi. Worked in the textile mills in Compton. Humble man and didn't have no enemies that nobody could account for. And Good Lord, after he died that little house of his and Miss Sarah's just filled up with people from front door to back. Couldn't find a place to sit if you came late. Lots of folks had to stand out in the yard! Miss Sarah had to come out and see *them* rather than the other way around. And oh the food! So many good smells coming from the kitchen and conflicting in a good way with one another. I never seen to beat at the meats and vegetables and pies and cakes! Lord, it was like we had all died and gone to heaven at the same time and was enjoying the endless bounty of God's great feast. We sat – those who could find places – and talked and ate and laughed and remembered all that was good about Ernest P. Freeman, and those memories were as plentiful as the food that crammed Miss Sarah's little kitchen.

There was just one distraction, one thing that didn't quite sit right with me and some others who attended the wake. It was when Semona Diggs showed up – poof! – like out of nowhere and dressed like I do not know what. In sneaker shoes and a long brown coat that touched the tops of them. A trench coat maybe? Like Columbo from the TV show but longer. She looked like a girl-child standing in the middle of everything. Didn't have one wrinkle to show on her face, and she had to be more than sixty years old. Wore a brown wig too that came down on her forehead in straight bangs. She kind of looked like a little black doll baby wrapped up in that big coat. And she just stood around blinking at everybody, like it was us that had shown up as a crowd at *her* house.

"What's wrong with her?" Delicia Baker said next to me. We were both standing with plates of food in our hands, hoping a couple of chairs would open up so we could enjoy the food and not have it run all the way down to our feet. Delicia never did care much for Semona, although I never knew exactly what the source of the dislike was. Sometimes there is no clear reason for these things. Sometimes a person just rubs you the wrong way, even if they don't mean to. The way they dress. How they talk. It's all wrong, wrong, wrong, somehow or other. Just them being alive the same time as you irritates the devil out of you. I suspect that's what it was with Delicia and Semona. Natural enemies. Like cat and dog.

"You think she got on anything underneath that coat?" Dee went on. "Maybe she don't have nothing nice enough to wear to a wake. Just threw a coat over her old naked body and came on."

I laughed and said, "Lord Jesus, if she is naked, I sure hope that coat don't fall open."

"If she is naked, maybe she ought to go up to Mr. Freeman and flash him. Might scare him up from his coffin."

Delicia is the kind of person that when she gets something in her head, she does not let go of it that easily. And she got it in her head that evening that she was going to embarrass and humiliate old Semona Diggs in front of everybody, irregardless of the real reason for us being there.

It didn't take too much longer.

Semona made like she was going to leave. Delicia spotted her and followed her the best she could, edging past folks, squeezing in her shoulders, so she wouldn't bump too much into other people. Finally the two of them had reached a fairly clear spot in the front room of Miss Sarah's house. Semona kept moving toward the door, just rocking back and forth on her sneakered feet, looking every bit like a child or a duck or a penguin or a something else besides a grown woman in her sixties. That's when Delicia made her move.

"Miss Semona! Oh Miss Semona!" she called out, like she was about to draw Semona's attention to the fact that she had left something behind.

"Yes?" Semona said long and slow as she turned back.

They faced each other. Delicia smiled big. She put out her hand for the left shoulder of Semona's coat and gave a hard jerk. Semona had been holding it closed with only one hand, so the younger, stronger woman had no trouble getting it open.

It was the blamedest thing I'd ever seen.

Inside the lining of Semona's coat were pockets, deep ones, on each side and lined up in horizontal rows. And in each of the pockets was food – meats and cheeses wrapped in paper towels, a whole loaf of bread, cake and cookies in tinfoil, even a bottle of ketchup in one hiding place. I knew all this because Delicia, who had not only stopped Semona in her tracks but also stunned her there with her boldness, did a fast little inventory of what she found. She took out each parcel and laid it on a nearby table till the coat was empty and Semona stood with a face turned to stone from embarrassment.

Delicia laughed so hard she leaned back on her heels.

"Why, Miss Semona! I didn't know you ran a grocery store out of your coat! Reckon I ought to start shopping with you instead of Bi-Lo. You take coupons?"

Semona mumbled something under her breath.

"Ma'am?" Delicia asked her.

That's when Semona spoke up very clearly, so nobody standing there would mistake what she said.

"It ain't none of your business what I do!"

Delicia cocked her head to one shoulder and grinned with one side of her mouth.

"I hear you do a lot of this, Miss Semona. Steal food from dead people."

"It ain't stealing! It's put out to eat, ain't it? How is that stealing?"

"I don't know, ma'am. You the one hiding food in your coat."

By this time somebody had gone and got Miss Sarah, Ernest Freeman's widow.

"It's all right, Semona," Miss Sarah said. "Take it. They's plenty left." And she even went to the table where Delicia had deposited the food and picked everything up and put it back in Semona's coat herself and gave Semona's shoulder a squeeze.

Nothing else was said about it – that night anyway.

Mama hadn't gone to Mr. Freeman's wake. She had had to work that night. But she caught word of it.

"Y'all ought to be ashamed," she said later, kind of catching me off guard.

"Don't say 'y'all'!" I told her. "'Y'all' didn't do anything. It was Dee that yanked open Semona's coat."

"I feel sure, Jasmine, you were right there with her in spirit if nothing else. Y'all not poor like Semona. Y'all have never wanted for nothing. Y'all not old either. But you will be one day. If you lucky, that is."

Getting caught like she did at Ernest Freeman's wake did not stop Semona Diggs' squirrel-like behavior of taking other people's food and hiding it away. Now I wasn't at the home-viewing of everybody who passed in Beaslap at that time. Nor did I attend all the funerals and then go back to the deceased's home place for refreshments because I wasn't kin to nor did I know all of them. But I was present at a good many of them, and without fail Semona Diggs showed too.

By then she had given up her secret agent costume of the long, tiered coat. She just shamelessly waddled out of the house loaded down with plates of food, whether it was the food of people she knew or not, and mostly it was the latter. Nobody said a word to her about it either, just stood and watched as she went her way. And if I wasn't there to witness this myself, I got reports from others who did, mostly Dee Baker, who did seem to be kin to or to know almost everybody in the southeastern corner of Compton County. It just burned her up to see it happen, even more than it did me.

"That heifer," she said once when we just happened to get on the topic. "If she knew those folks, if she cared anything about 'em, it wouldn't make me so mad. But she don't. She's just using everybody, especially the loved ones."

"She's a user and a loser," I chimed in.

"She mean as the devil. That's for sure."

"I know that's right." We sat and thought a minute, the both of us. Then I said. "I wonder who will go see Somona when she dies?"

Dee smiled then answered: "Nobody. The devil that comes to get her. The undertaker. The preacher. Maybe. If they can find one Semona hadn't bad-mouthed."

It was a funny and strange thing that we would have that conversation, because not more than a month later the news came that Semona Diggs herself had died. She hadn't been out of her house in days. A neighbor, brave enough, had gone snooping around Semona's house then had gone running to her telephone to call 911, because, she said, she had spotted Semona flat on her back in her bedroom, her eyes wide open like she was inspecting her ceiling for cracks or bugs. This woman called and called to her, but Semona never responded.

There was no viewing of her body at the house or at the church she attended now or at the funeral home – just a graveside service. The announcement of her passing and burial got a small write-up in the paper. That's how I knew about it. You see, Dee Baker didn't go to see Semona buried, but I did. I don't know why. Curiosity mostly, I reckon. Just to see who else might show up, to answer that question me and Dee had posed to each other a month back. And it wasn't many. The minister, like we predicted, and a few others. What family she had or those of her family who still cared. Some cousins from North Carolina, I believe, if the newspaper was right. It was sad, the saddest funeral I ever went to. The minister didn't know what to say about Semona. (Who would have?) He just read a lot of familiar Bible passages about death and rebirth just to fill up the time. A lady in a dark blue dress stepped forward and sang "Just As I am" acapella in a voice that creaked and cracked. And then with nothing else said, they buried Semona in the ground and piled dirt on her. I tell you what: it was the strangest thing, because as the dirt was piled on, I reached up my hands to my face and found tears there. I was crying for Semona Diggs! A lady I had spent years making fun of. I wiped the tears away and said to myself, "Oh it's a funeral. Everybody cries at funerals. Don't matter who it is dead and getting buried." But it was more than that. I just thought about her dying all by herself in that little house and how when she was alive all she cared about was getting other people's food into that house. Again, she reminded me of a squirrel that spends all its time and energy storing up nuts for the winter time. She could be mean as a snake, yes, but…was that the worst thing a human being could be accused of, taking food that had been offered free in the first place?

I didn't let anybody know I went to the service.

And then a few days later the strangest thing of all in this whole story happened.

Delicia Baker called me, all upset, just a-crying, so much so I couldn't really understand what she was saying at first.

"Ah Jasmine, you the only one I can tell this to. The only one."

"Tell me what? Calm down. Get yourself together. Tell me what?"

She paused to get her crying under control, reduced it to some sniffles, then said just as plain as if she might be telling me what kind of weather we had outside: "I killed Semona Diggs."

I didn't say anything.

After a few minutes she said, "Did you hear me, Jasmine?"

I still didn't say anything.

"I said I killed Semona Diggs."

Then I broke out laughing.

"Lord Dee, you got a crazy sense of humor, calling somebody up and saying something like that! You killed somebody. You got to crack some funnier jokes than that if you want to stay friends with me!" And I just laughed again but was the only one on the phone laughing right then.

"I ain't joking!"

My mouth went dry and my head began to spin just a little. "What you talking about, Dee? Semona had a heart attack. That's what the coroner said. You can't make no heart attack."

She kind of spit out a little laugh.

"Sure you can. You can scare somebody to death."

Without any more fuss or questions, she began to tell how in her mind she had killed Semona Diggs.

It was supposed to be a joke mainly. Just a way for Dee to satisfy herself that she had hit back some at that mean old thief Semona. Just a way maybe to teach Semona a lesson, get her to change her way, being a little less using of grieving folks.

Late at night, real late, Dee and her sister LaKenya sneaked up to and around Semona's house. Semona kept no dog near her to warn her of strangers on her property. She didn't have an alarm system. None of that. Her place was innocent and open that night. The moon was out and full-bright. Shadows ran long and black everywhere. It was quiet and chilly and just a perfect night for this kind of mischief. The sisters had dressed themselves in black tee-shirts and dark jeans. Dee had on a Freddy Krueger mask she got at Spencer's in Spartanburg one time. LaKenya had on the mask of a lady vampire. They crept around the doors and windows of the house, trying to find a way inside. The house was old and flimsy and hadn't been painted or worked on, at least the outside, since it was first put in, nobody knows when. Dee said she probably could have removed part of the wall with her bare hands and gone in that way. To both of their surprise, they found the front door wasn't locked, so they just went on in.

"What if Semona had been waiting with a gun, Dee?" I interrupted her. "What would you have done then?"

"Got shot, I reckon," Dee answered me and went on with her story.

They moved quiet as little mice into the house. With help from all the moonlight pouring in, they could see pretty good around them, and what they saw was how bare Semona's house was. There wasn't much danger of banging into furniture in the dark, because there wasn't much furniture to speak of. Dee said it was about as empty as a cell in the county jail. Maybe more so. They saw one or two hardback chairs. No couch. And there was a knickknack shelf that was empty except for an electric lamp on top of it. She said that she and LaKenya had the exact same thought at the exact same time, and that was that Semona Diggs *really was poor*, or if she had anything she had it well-hidden away in some other part of the house.

They had gone too far into the house to change their plans. In fact, they didn't really have a plan. They were there to scare Miss Semona and to make her think twice about going to dead folks' houses to take advantage of them. Turned out, they didn't need a plan. Things just kind of worked out for them. Stepping carefully further into the house, Dee put her foot down on the floor. Semona had no carpet there or rug, just the wood the place had been built with so many years ago. The floorboard creaked loud. It moaned like a lady in distress and scared Dee and LaKenya. They grabbed onto each other. That's when Semona cried out from the next room just in front of them.

"Who's there?"

The sisters didn't say anything right away.

"Best get gone, whoever you are, lessen you want to say hello to the police!"

Dee said it was time to get the show on the road.

"Ooooooooooh!" she started, just like any ghost would, I reckon.

"Who is it?" Semona said into the dark.

"It's Sally Williams from the Old Hope Road," Dee said in a voice she tried to make low and scary.

"She dead. Been dead for ten years."

"I'm back now, Semona Diggs, and I brought others with me." And that's when she and LaKenya called out the names of the deceased in as many made-up voices they could manage.

"Ernest Freeman."

"Mamie Robinson."

"Gloria Gossett."

"Maddy Rice."

"Betty Ruth Gist."

"Clemont Perry, Jr."

And others. They continued to name the recent dead.

"But y'all gone!" Semona hollered from her room behind the wall, her bedroom Dee figured. "Y'all dead!"

"We back now. To get what belongs to us."

"What is that?"

"Gimme back my roasted chicken!"

"Gimme back my tater salad!"

"I want my cracklin' cornbread."

"My lima beans!"

"My chitlins!"

"My nanner puddin'!"

"I can't give it back. It's all gone. Long gone."

"Then we'll take you instead, Semona Diggs!"

That's when Dee heard Semona's bed creaking, or whatever it was, and Semona coming closer to the doorway. Dee figured she better make her big move and get gone. So to prevent Semona coming out into the den, Dee leaped in the doorway and growled like some monstrous beast. She had on that Freddie Krueger mask. She saw Semona in her nightgown take several steps back from the door. She had seen Dee in her get-up floating through the dark now towards her. Her mouth dropped open. Both her hands went to it. She was trying to say something or to scream. LaKenya laughed behind Dee, which got Dee tickled. LaKenya turned for the front door. Dee followed her. They ran into the cool quiet night just a-snickering.

"You don't know if that's what killed Semona."

"What else could it be?"

"She was old. And she sure didn't eat like she should have. Anything could have took her out."

"Oh please Jasmine. You know better than that."

"No ma'am, I really don't. I'm not a doctor or a coroner or anything like that. And neither are you."

That was all the comfort I could give Delicia right then, because I truly could not say what happened to Semona Diggs, what killed her other than her own bad heart. Of course I wouldn't say anything to anybody else if Dee didn't want me to. What would be the point? What I couldn't help but do, and this was while I was still on the phone with Dee, was to think how both of us, Dee and me, had our own secrets regarding Semona Diggs. Dee had gone to her house at night dressed like a boogeyman set out to teach her some kind of lesson. I had gone to her funeral but had stood as far away from Semona and her family and the minister as I could and still see what was going on, afraid I'd be spotted and accused of pitying Semona Diggs, of *caring* about her when for so long I had led the laughers and the haters against Semona. I wanted to let all that off my chest right then, to tell Dee, but I couldn't.

In a strange moment, it was like what I had done to Semona was the worst of the two things.

Mae Ola: A Remonstrance

You just love to worry, don't you?

Wallow in worrying, I say.

I never seen nobody study worrying the way you do. Looking for every opportunity they are to have your nerves tore up.

How come?

You say you didn't start till Daddy died, that it was his passing what set you off, but I know that ain't true. It begun way before then.

Every noise – every bad piece of news – every forecast of rain and thunder – sets you to shuddering like a chihuhua dog that's been yelled at.

And I'm talking about bad stuff you see on the TV, not what's happening in your own back yard. Bad stuff that goes on someplace else – Gaffney, Spartanburg, here, there – and not where we live. They predict a tornado in Tulsa, Oklahoma, and you go running to the bathroom to lock yourself in it, like they's honest chance that bad wind is going spin itself all the way over to South Carolina. A crazy man breaks out of jail in Greenville, and you lock all the doors and windows, like he's headed straight for 101 Charlestown Court and no place else.

Your health is good. You strong as an ox. Smart as a whip. Ain't got the sugar or the Oldtimey's, and here you are – what? – eighty-three years old.

What is it makes some women go on like that?

Is it the curse of Eve?

But that was the curse of blood we all have.

The shame of nakedness.

You tried to explain once: how you growed up in the country and that give you a fear of what the Lord made – the wind, the lighting, the driving rain, the beast in the woods, the very ugly heart of mankind. Some such as that. And you said it was the right and proper thing to be – afraid in the Lord. But it ain't fear of the Lord. It's the plain fear of living.

The Lord put us here to live. Why else?

For a long time, it got to where you wouldn't even leave the house. Become a shut-in. Got Daddy to worrying about you as much as you worried about yourself. (Oh, I ain't going to say his worrying killed him. Won't put that burden on you. But it played a part, I'm willing to bet.)

He done everything he knowed to do.

Had the women from your Sunday school class come to see you, talk to you, pray for you, invite you back to church, to the circle meetings. But you told them no. Even said to their faces how you wasn't sure the Lord meant you to be happy, that maybe some folks He has circled out just to be miserable. And they never come again, and who'd blame them? A waste of time getting you to see the light.

Had the doctor write you a prescription for depression pills. You took them once, twice then stopped. Didn't give them time to work. Said they made you feel bloated, itchy, that you just itched yourself red and raw in one place.

Then he planted the flower garden for you. Planted it in spring and by summer had the front yard ablaze with zinnia and 'zaleas, nasturtiums and calla lilies and goodness knows what else. There was so much color in that front yard, it was like he had set a bonfire to the grass. When he had it good and going, he turned to you and said it was yours to take care of now, that it was good for the body and the mind to work the ground, to be among so much color and so much natural life. You went out to it twice, stood out in it for only a few minutes then turned and come back in and never paid it no more mind.

Then Daddy died. A heart attack. He was out in the yard, near the flower garden he'd made just for you, when he dropped just like that. Dead by the time he hit the ground.

Oh, I ain't blaming you for him dying. No ma'am. But I'd be lying if I didn't say he died from a broken heart rather than a busted one. It was like you rejected Daddy when you rejected the garden he had built up for you. Like you turned away a child that come from his flesh, his loins, one he wanted to join to your flesh, but you wouldn't have it. He offered it, and you done what? Come back into this house, to this chair, to wait and worry away what's left of your life.

Him dying give you the excuse you was looking for, hoping for all these long years.

The only thing that would make it better would be for me to fall down in the pit with you and wallow just as hard.

But I won't. Never have. Never will. You wonder why I don't come here to see you much no more. Why I don't bring the grandyounguns round no more. Look in the mirror, honey. Ought to be clear as day to you by now. They's more fun to be had in the cemetery than in coming here. In fact, that is where we go – where I go – to see Daddy, planted in the earth like the force of life he put in the ground right outside your front door, which you then proceeded to let die after Daddy died. I talk to him now and shake my head and tell him I know he wants me to look after you, and I try, but there ain't no way to live for nobody else. It's a sure way to hurry up your own death.

And then I come here and see you there all drawed up like you got the weight of the world on you, when of course you don't, and I want to lift up both of my hands together, in one big old fist, and hit you and hit you and hit you like I'm striking a dying heart to get it beating again and full of blood and hope that will bring some spirit back to you, return to you, whatever life you might have had a long time ago. But I don't hit you, of course. And I won't. Never. Because I'll be durned if I give up my own life trying to get your life back to you.

Old Man's Burden

Mr. Newhouse's daughter in Atlanta no longer knew what to do about her younger son, Kyle. He was completely out of control. He violated curfew regularly. He cultivated distasteful friends and assumed their worst characteristics and generally behaved with unwarranted sullenness and disrespect. He had been given *everything*, after all: a private school education, trips, without a chaperone, to places like New York and Chicago, even a shiny-gold Maserati shortly after he had attained his permanent driver's license. How could he react with such ingratitude – his name in the paper for vandalism of public property in Grant Park, his arrest for the taunting of an elderly homeless man in Mid-town, and simply the worrying provoked by his new recklessness – ?

Mrs. Blackburn, Mr. Newhouse's daughter, concluded reasonably that living in Atlanta (the suburb of Lawrenceville exactly) only exacerbated the problem, what with the myriad temptations and opportunities offered by the city. So she decided, without consultation with anyone else, including her father, to move the young man to a smaller place for a while. A place like Compton, South Carolina, where she herself had grown up, might work some change in the boy's attitude. Compton was no Atlanta, for sure, wasn't even a fifth Atlanta's size (this she calculated without aid of a map) and therefore had to be insulated from much, if not most, of the ugliness and corruption that adhere to urban areas like Atlanta and its suburbs. She believed that in her heart if not her head. After all, Compton had barely come into the twentieth century, and here it was the twenty-first. People still kept their doors unlocked day and night (so Mrs. Blackburn supposed, as that had been a practice during her girlhood). They greeted each other in the streets without suspicion. They went to church frequently and proudly. They still voted for Democrats in state and local elections, surely a sign of naiveté which indicated child-like innocence.

"Daddy," Mrs. Blackburn addressed her father on the phone shortly after conceiving this idea. "I want Kyle to come stay with you in Compton this summer. It'll do him good. It'll do everybody good. What's wrong with him? He's a rascal! Haven't I told you? Oh I have. Yes. You just haven't been listening, Daddy. Do you just not care? I want him to come stay with you and learn to be a gentleman. Yes, that's right. Well, here's your chance to make one exist. What? Put him to work. Put him in the restaurant. Put him in your yard. Make him appreciate all he's been given. I can't imagine your being without any resources in that regard. I know, Daddy, you only raised girls. How well I know, being one of the girls you raised. But I trust you in this. You hear me? I trust you!"

Mr. Newhouse hung up the telephone, confused and disappointed. He really didn't like his daughter's idea and hoped that the irrefutable fact of his having raised only females, Mrs. Blackburn, of course, and her Charleston-residing sister, would dissuade her. But she did not take no for an answer. In fact, she did not even give him a chance to answer one way or the other. She had made up his mind for him, and thus followed a flurry of emails from Atlanta, from Mrs. Blackburn, specifying and reiterating Kyle's behavioral oddities and her suggestions for mastering them: early rising, a solid diet, regular exercise, etc. (Mr. Newhouse did not receive the emails himself, having no computer savvy, but relied on an employee to retrieve them, print them out, and answer them if an answer were warranted.)

Mr. Newhouse, having thus been railroaded by his daughter, could only sit and ponder the situation with bemusement. What was wrong, after all, with being a rascal and a rebel? Wasn't rebellious rascality not a natural part of being a normal boy? Goodness knows he, Winthrop Newhouse, had been both rascal and rebel, and look where it had gotten him: in a two million dollar mansion smack dab in the middle of Main Street and a business that brought in after taxes, in excess of five million dollars annually. He could not have achieved any of that if he had not been a rebel and somewhat of an s.o.b. at times. That's because he had had to fight for everything he had. Nothing had been given to him. He had not been brought up in a family of affluence; he had not inherited wealth or his business. He had been reared in the sticks, literally, the son of what could only be termed "white trash" – a term he himself used almost proudly in describing his family. As a boy, he had been laughed at for his patched clothing and his school lunches of sardines and "sody" crackers. Nobody expected anything else from him but penury and ignominy.

Instead of capitulating to them, Mr. Newhouse used their scorn and indifference as building blocks – first, for a flourishing peach orchard, one of the most successful in the South Carolina upcountry, later, for Winner's Circle, the fast food restaurant that had not only existed but thrived for more than forty years, outlasting all other such locally owned restaurants. In the meantime, he had remodeled then moved into the two story house on South Main, a gorgeous white edifice with a vast front porch and thick Doric columns, all guarded over by towering, glistening magnolias. A vintage Roadster sat in the marble carport. At one point his late wife Virginia had gone through three Cadillacs in five years. And both his daughters had attended two of the finest colleges in the state, Converse and The College of Charleston. He even ventured out of the business realm into politics, running for elected office as a Republican in the face of the overwhelming Compton Democratic establishment – and nearly won.

Nobody laughed at Winthrop Newhouse anymore. At least not to his face.

So Mr. Newhouse took it as a point of pride that he had a rebellious grandson, a "chip off the old block," as the cliché had it, without really understanding the nature of Kyle's rebellion. Yes, he remembered vaguely Mrs. Blackburn's accounts of the boy's misbehavior, but he accepted it all as signs of natural adolescent rambunctiousness, nothing serious, nothing to be out of sorts about. My God, if women didn't worry themselves about the least little thing! And usually it amounted to nothing at all.

So it was with a sense of resigned weariness that Mr. Newhouse met the day of his grandson's arrival in South Carolina. Linda Bishop, the middle-aged black lady who cooked and cleaned for him four days out of the weak, prepared him a stout breakfast: bacon, eggs, grits, toast, and jam, which Mr. Newhouse washed down with cup after cup of hot black coffee.

"You nervous about meeting this boy?" Mrs. Bishop asked him as he crouched over his meal.

Mr. Newhouse eyed her as though she had just sworn at him. "No ma'am. I'm too old and too mean to be nervous about anything."

"That so? Well, something must be going on with you. You took a day off from work. That don't happen very often. Fact of business, I started to call the newspaper and TV and let them know, for surely this is news in Compton, South Carolina."

Mr. Newhouse responded by flinging back the remnants of his coffee and setting the cup down with a pronounced thud. But Mrs. Bishop had a point. In the more than forty years since he had been running Winner's Circle, he only took off one week for vacation, shutting down the restaurant for that week, knowing he could trust no one else to run it properly. He and Mrs. Newhouse usually spent the week in Myrtle Beach or Gatlinburg. But Mrs. Newhouse was gone now and Mr. Newhouse had consequently lost his taste for travel. He should have gone to Atlanta or Charleston to see either of his daughters and her family, but more and more he spent that vacation week at home, occasionally taking a fishing trip with an acquaintance.

Mrs. Bishop had left the dining room but quickly returned. Her face beamed.

"If I'm not mistaken," she said, her voice almost sing-songy, "you got company pulling in your front yard."

Together they went to the door and watched the sleek black SUV as it sat silently in the driveway. The late spring morning was bright and already warm, the clear blue sky sizzling.

"Well, are they getting out or not?" Mrs. Bishop asked, and as though she had been heard by the car's occupants, the two front doors of the SUV flew open swiftly together, like wings spreading on a roc. The first to emerge was Mrs. Blackburn, Darlene, Mr. Newhouse's elder daughter, in her mid-fifties now but still resplendently blonde like her late mother, her hair piled on her head and complemented by her white blouse and black, knee-length skirt and the long black scarf bound at her throat.

"Hey Daddy!" she called upon seeing her father on the wide front porch. She went to him and bound him in her arms. He felt suffocated, more by her perfume than her hug, but he did his best to show sufficient affection with small, slow pats on her stiff back. Over her shoulder he watched the second passenger leave the vehicle and became perplexed. At first, from the boy's long, unkempt blond hair, sealed in place by a ball cap, he thought Kyle was a girl.

"That him?" he said, prying himself loose from Mrs. Blackburn's grip and breathing regularly again.

His daughter turned and smiled. "Yes! Kyle! Come up and see your Pa-Pa. You sat on his knee the last time you were here. Look at him, Daddy! That big boy of ours. Fifteen years old now!"

The boy did not immediately respond to his mother's call. He stood in place by the SUV, and this gave his grandfather the opportunity to survey him more completely. He wore a blue and white ball cap turned backwards. Wisps of fair bangs escaped the cap's brim. His small frame was hidden by a long basketball jersey which hung out of his pants and reached nearly to his knees. His pants were jeans, and they slouched so low on him they threatened to drop to his feet. His feet were shod in bright white sneakers with the word *Scarface* prominent on each tongue.

"Is there something wrong with him?" Mr. Newhouse asked.

Mrs. Blackburn looked at her father in alarm. "What do you mean?"

"The way he's dressed."

Mrs. Blackburn laughed. "That's the way the young dress nowadays. Oh Daddy, you run a restaurant. You see all types. Surely you've seen young people come in dressed that way."

"If I have, I looked away real quick."

"Well, see there. That will be part of your mission. To get him to dress the way a conservative young man should dress."

"I reckon." Mr. Newhouse watched the idling boy further. "Is he slow?"

"Slow? You mean – ? Daddy, why?"

"He just stands there. He don't move. Even after you called him."

By now the boy had removed a Blackberry from one voluminous front pants pocket and was speaking into it."

"Oh Good Lord."

"Kyle, put that away and come speak to your granddaddy. He's been standing here the longest waiting on you." Mrs. Blackburn turned back to her father. "Don't worry, Daddy. He's to have only the phone. No video games or other mechanical devices. Only two hours of TV a day. Keep it on Fox News as much you can. That should keep his head straight. And oh yes! He's too young for tattoos and piercings, so don't worry about 'body art.'"

"I'm not," Newhouse replied. "And I don't own a TV."

Kyle Blackburn, as though from defiance, continued to talk into the phone before pulling it away from his ear and pushing a button to kill the signal. He looked dead-eye at the porch, directly at his mother and grandfather, with something of the predatory in his gaze. Finally he took measured steps toward the house, and when he reached the porch's first step, he jerked his chin upward abruptly and said, "What up?"

Newhouse eyed him from head to foot and replied, "Not your britches, that's for sure. If you're not careful, son, you're going to trip over yourself."

"Kyle, come up here and shake your granddaddy's hand the way a young gentleman would."

"Yo," replied the youngster." "I ain't no gentleman, young or old –"

"That's obvious," Newhouse slipped in.

"– when you come from the streets of Atlanta like I do, you don't just give out your handshake like candy. The other thug got to earn your respect. Then you shake. You read me?"

"Stop talking like a cartoon and come give your grandfather a proper greeting."

The boy moved closer, within touching range of Winthrop Newhouse, and extended his right arm, at the end of which stood a balled fist.

After a second of staring, Mr. Newhouse said, "Okay, and what am I supposed to do with *that*?"

"Fist bump. Yo, you read me?"

Mr. Newhouse took a damask-backed chair in his ornately furnished dining room, joined by Linda Bishop, the two of them amazed at the fact that Kyle Blackburn aided his mother in removing his things from the SUV and transferring them to the upstairs bedroom which had once served as Mrs. Blackburn's own when she was a teenager.

Mr. Newhouse regarded it all with the same kind of calm that the citizens of conquered nations in great wars must feel when their houses are confiscated by their conquerors.

"Mr. Newhouse," Mrs. Bishop said, "you know what you got on your hands with Mr. Kyle Blackburn yonder?"

"I got some idea, Linda, but I'm open to other suggestions."

Mrs. Bishop summoned a long breath then said, "A wigger."

Newhouse paused then said, "A what?"

Mrs. Bishop repeated the term.

"What in the hell's a wigger, Linda?"

Mrs. Bishop drew a second long breath before saying, "A white n —"

"Excuse me?"

"A white n — "

"Ma'am?"

Mrs. Bishop sighed. "A white n-word. The n-word. Lord, some folks has a time catching on!"

"Oh you mean a white nig —"

"Yes!" Mrs. Bishop fairly shouted, rolling her eyes to the ceiling, thankful she had been able to arrest the word before it had been fully enunciated. "That's what I mean."

"But what do you mean by what you mean?"

"It's a white boy thinks he's black."

"Oh."

"I cannot believe you are unacquainted with wiggers. You run a restaurant after all. A public place. The wiggers are in and out of it all the time."

"I choose to ignore what does not please me."

"No. You color blind to all the colors except *green*. Like the green of a dollar bill."

Mr. Newhouse smiled.

A clamor sounded suddenly on the stairs. Mrs. Blackburn and Kyle were descending. "Daddy? Where'd you get to?" Mrs. Blackburn giggled.

Newhouse said nothing; neither did Mrs. Bishop. They allowed mother and son to discover them.

"There you are!" Mrs. Blackburn exclaimed. Kyle stood beside her, sullen, pants still perched precipitously on his small hips. "Daddy, do you know what Kyle said about your house?" She raised an index finger. "One word. *Sick*. He said it was *sick*." And she giggled again to the point of giddiness, like a tourist guide delighted by her job.

Linda Bishop nudged Newhouse. "Believe it or not, that's a good thing."

"Glad to know it," he said.

"But," Mrs. Blackburn went on, "by the time Kyle leaves here, Daddy, I trust he'll be saying it's healthy. Or wonderful. Or beautiful. Or whatever a gentleman would say about a grand place such as this." She then went into an impromptu history of the house for the benefit of her son. She told him that originally their family had lived in a similar place in the Beaslap section of Compton County until it burned down (the house, that is, not Beaslap). Then they moved into town to this house, which had once belonged to an old cotton mill boss named J. Vaughan Hemphill, who had passed away. The boy stood as stone-silent as he had before his mother had made clear these origins. Maybe he *had* meant *sick* in the traditional sense and wanted nothing to do with the house.

After Darlene Blackburn's departure for Atlanta, Linda Bishop prepared an excellent supper for Winthrop Newhouse and his grandson: sliced roast beef, squash casserole, scarlet potatoes, hot buttered biscuits, and sweet iced tea. Mr. Newhouse ate the meal with quiet appreciation, even some gusto, as if to show the younger man what an authentic South Carolina "gentlemanly" appetite looked like. And it was genuine, for he had grown up very poor and had been lucky when he was a boy if he got any supper at all. In memory of such lean times, he always left a clean plate.

Kyle Blackburn, however, had not grown up poor. He ignored the food in front of him, concentrating instead on his Blackberry, pushing the numbers frantically. His head was lowered, his lips pursed, a bit of blond hair escaped the brim of his hat. Mr. Newhouse watched him and could not help but notice a resemblance to both the boy's mother and his grandmother – the fair skin, the firm lines of his face, the clear blue of his eyes (when they were visible.)

"Something wrong with your supper?" he finally asked.

The boy took a moment, still engaged in texting, before he raised his head and shook it.

Linda Bishop appeared at the dining room door.

"You know if a man wears a hat in the house, he'll go bald-headed before he's twenty."

Kyle shot her a look of alarm then said, "That's a'ight. I plan to shave my head anyway. A true thug goes shiny."

"And what in the world's the matter with that roast beef, mister? That's a meal fit for a king."

"Give it to the king then. Y'all got a Mickey D's around here?"

Linda Bishop cleared her throat and said to Mr. Newhouse, "He means McDonald's."

"Somehow I got that one," Newhouse replied, "and it scares me a little bit."

The next morning, to Mr. Newhouse's surprise, Kyle Blackburn showed at breakfast dressed like an actual young man, in a green polo shirt and chino slacks. The cap was gone. The boy had unleashed his fine blond hair, and once again Mr. Newhouse thought of both his fair-haired daughters and their blond mother. He was good-looking, no doubt. Mr. Newhouse could not help but feel some measure of pride. Then he wondered what deal Darlene, Mrs. Blackburn, had struck with the boy to "clean up." What had she promised to buy him? He even ate the eggs and bacon put in front of him without criticism and only brought out his Blackberry once and briefly. A miracle already? This soon? Mr. Newhouse would wait and see.

The boy rode to Winner's Circle with Mr. Newhouse in Mr. Newhouse's red pick-up truck. Mr. Newhouse did not put Kyle to work that very first day, but his plan, such as he had come up with one, was eventually to have the boy do something in the restaurant – wash dishes, sweep, fill ketchup bottles. But that first day Kyle took a table in the restaurant's far corner and spent it not observing the flow of customers or the routines of his grandfather's employees but engaged with his gadget, his Blackberry, whose keys he worked with the swift magic of an old-fashioned cotton weaver on shuttles. Mr. Newhouse could not help feel some disappointment. He went over to the boy a couple of times in hopes of interesting him in what went on around him but to no avail. At five o'clock he drove the boy back to his home on Main Street where Mrs. Bishop kept supper warm in the oven.

The next day, and those following, he found Kyle Blackburn no more intrigued with Winner's Circle than he had been the first days. The phone kept the young man's full attention. Soon Mr. Newhouse felt the prick of frustration, rejection even. He even grew a bit angry, so much so, at some point he left the front counter, where normally he guarded the cash register like a one-eyed hawk, to phone his daughter in Atlanta.

"Take it away from him, Daddy," Mrs. Blackburn insisted upon hearing of the present dilemma. "Yes. Take it. Right this minute. And put him to work. You're not afraid to, are you?"

Hanging up the phone, Mr. Newhouse went directly to the booth where his grandson sat and held out his hand.

The boy squinted his eyes. His mouth became a hard line. Then he said, "Yo, what's up?"

"Give me that phone."

The boy's eyes narrowed further. "What? You got to make a phone call or something? Ain't you got your own phone, you being a big boss man and all? Yo, yo." And he laughed.

"Your mama said to take it from you. So I'm taking it. And putting you to work today. You'll operate the dishwasher."

"Now hold on here, boss man. This here's my lifeline to the homies back in the big ATL. I lose this, I lose everything. Now I done put on these monkey clothes that I wouldn't be seen dead in in Hotlanta. That ought to be enough civilizing for one summer vacation. Don't you think?"

In a move that surprised even himself, Mr. Newhouse reached out swiftly and snatched the phone from the boy's hand. "I got an apron for you back yonder. Go put it on."

As Mr. Newhouse expected, the boy showed lank interest in his new duty. He stood by as one of the other employees showed him the simple operations of the dishwasher then did his very best to display abject ineptitude, the kind resulting in minor disruption of the restaurant's business flow. Mr. Newhouse grew agitated. He sent the boy out of the kitchen and had someone drive him back to the house.

Mr. Newhouse himself did not arrive home till very late that evening. It surprised him to see a downstairs window lit up at that hour. It was the window of his "study," the room he often went off to for greater relaxation – to have a drink if he wished or smoke a cigar or just sit and listen to the symphonic music which had become one of his pleasures of late. He entered the study first thing and experienced a second surprise: the sight of his grandson sitting at the vast oaken desk inlaid with glass and covered with memorabilia of various sorts.

"You old enough to smoke?" Mr. Newhouse asked Kyle Blackburn, who reclined in the swivel chair of rich leather holding aloft like a veteran smoker one of Mr. Newhouse's premium Don Carlos specialties.

"Since I was twelve years old, yo."

"Your mama would skin me and you both alive if she could see all this."

"Darlene's a hater. She hates what she don't understand. She don't understand me, so she hates me."

"That's the most ridiculous thing I've ever heard. She's given you everything. Probably too much."

"Ah, she buying me off, dog. That what she doing. Nice clothes. Trips everywhere. That a bribe, dog." The boy arched his eyebrows playfully and bit the tip of the cigar, still encased in its wrapping. He gave his grandfather the same squint as the day before. "You a hater too, ain't you, grandpa man?"

"What do you mean by that?"

The boy pointed behind him at the window, where hung suspended from the curtain rod was a St. Andrews Cross, a Confederate battle flag, a subject of intense controversy in South Carolina the last dozen years. "You're a hater. That's a sign of hate."

"I had kinfolk who fought and died under that flag. And you did too."

"I don't claim 'em as no kinfolk. They fought on the wrong side for the wrong thing. And it's a good thing they lost too."

"What would you know about it? Fifteen and all."

"Did you vote for Obama?"

"No."

"Hater."

"Get up from there and go to your own room right now."

"Ah chill out, dude. Let's make peace. Just pour us a drink and we'll toast. You got plenty of it. Some good stuff too."

"That'll be the day."

"And where did you get all them guns? You in the war too?"

The boy referred to Mr. Newhouse's collections of rifles and handguns, Winchesters and Gatlings among them, displayed on one wall of the study. The prized possession was a Confederate musket wielded by his great grandfather at Manassas, a British Enfield made in 1853, fifty-five inches and more than five pounds of accurate shot.

"Never mind that. Just go to bed. I'm tired of talking about things. It's late."

The boy set down the cigar, shaking his head slowly with the resignation of a grown man. "Ain't no love for a thug once he leave the ATL. Ain't no love in The Compton, South Carolina," he said and stood.

The next day was a regrettable replay of the previous one and initiated a most unfortunate new trend at Winner's Circle. Not only did Kyle Blackburn slough off his duties as dishwasher with indifference and ineptitude, finally abandoning the kitchen for the dining room and one of the restaurant booths, he also began attracting other like-minded youths, other "wiggers," Mr. Newhouse supposed, except these were white and black boys, slovenly dressed, loud, unmindful of other customers, some of them wearing ball caps, others bandannas, still others bedecked in long silver necklaces that reached as far as their stomachs, their ears glinting with rings, their mouths, some of them, with gold-capped teeth. Like Kyle, several of them had eschewed belts, so their pants hung precariously on their thin shanks. It was as though right away they recognized in Kyle Blackburn, a kindred soul, as though they had known each other a very long time, and he responded in kind. He even rose from his seat and embraced a couple of them in that peculiar young way, elbow blocking chest, chin squeezing shoulder. With alarm Mr. Newhouse wondered if these young men had come up from Atlanta to visit Kyle. But no. Kyle said he had just met them, that they were new "dogs," new "homies," that "a thug know a thug 'cause they got the same blood in 'em."

Mr. Newhouse did not ask for an elaboration of the last statement. He had no interest in hip-hop philosophy or genealogy. He became, however, greatly concerned for the atmosphere of Winner's Circle, because these young men returned daily, not always buying anything either, *usually* not buying anything, but certainly attracting Kyle's attention, luring him away from his job in the kitchen. They talked loudly and laughed loudly and drew the notice of paying customers who regarded this group of youths with something less than appreciation. It got to the point where Mr. Newhouse had to leave his post at the cash register and drive the boys outdoors, Kyle included. So outside they gathered, pulling up in the Winner's Circle parking lot in shiny cars with CD players blaring, thumping, thudding, shuddering, sending vibrations through the very interior of the restaurant itself. Kyle, of course, would dash out of the kitchen to join them and spend sometimes an hour or more with them, sharing drags off cigarettes and generally shooting the bull.

"You ought not to have done this to me," Mr. Newhouse told his daughter on the phone. "I'm too old to take a youngun to raise. I'm nearly eighty years old, Darlene. You know that."

"I'm sure you're doing a great job, Daddy. He's not wearing those awful clothes anymore, is he? Well, see there. That's progress. It's still early."

"I got a business to run. And my business ain't no daycare."

"I believe in you, Daddy. You're a tough old bird. You can do it."

To show how tough he was, Mr. Newhouse met the congregation of youths soon after they assembled in the parking lot one afternoon and told them they were no longer welcome on the grounds of Winner's Circle. They didn't buy anything and they caused problems. They were disturbing the peace in general and his customers specifically. If they returned, he would call the police. With the thump and sigh of a rap epic to score their departure, they left all together, abandoning Kyle, who stood and stared red-faced at his grandfather and said, "The world ain't nothing but a big ball of hate. You feel me?"

Mr. Newhouse wanted to say, "I'd like to feel my hand on your backside, again and again and again," but he didn't. He merely walked away from the boy and back to the cash register.

Kyle Blackburn did not accompany Mr. Newhouse to Winner's Circle the next day; he did not respond to his grandfather's calls to get out of bed. And he did not call in later to report the reason for his absence as any good employee would have. He repeated this "no show" the next few days, and in a way Mr. Newhouse was glad about it. It was a relief to him not to have to keep an eye on the boy. He could concentrate on the really important thing, the operation of Winner's Circle. It had been his daughter's mistake, this whole idea. Kyle would have to go back to Atlanta. Mr. Newhouse couldn't change him. He was obstinate. He would just have to grow out of this behavior, if that were possible.

One evening shortly after that, Mr. Newhouse closed up the restaurant by himself. It was very late, past one o'clock in the morning. It had been a long day, very hard, and it was the first time in a long while that Mr. Newhouse regretted that he did not have an obvious candidate, male or female, to whom he could turn over operations of Winner's Circle. He had no family in town. His younger brother Marvin, who never married and had no children himself, had died of The Old Timey's disease years ago in a nursing home in Greenwood, South Carolina. His wife was gone, and both his daughters had fled to big cities to raise their own families, none of whom had any interest in returning to a small place like Compton. For a while he thought of Kyle and what a waste it was the boy did not have his head on straight, at least not at the moment. Maybe if he did, a few years from then...but no, there was no cause for hope there either.

He pondered these things as he rode home in the silent darkness of the little town, tired but still edgy, and as he neared his own home, he was startled to find it the scene of great activity so late in the night and early in the morning. A Compton County police squad car sat in the driveway, blue lights skittering from one end of the roof to the other. So did other cars. Perhaps a dozen or nearly so, parked in the drive, on the curb, on the lawn. The house itself was fully lit from top floor to bottom, each window ablaze. Mr. Newhouse parked on the curb opposite his home and rushed out of the truck, not even bothering to remove the keys from the ignition. He scurried up the drive, onto the porch, and into the house. Two young deputies stood in the foyer talking to a pair of black youths. Other young men, black and white, lingered nearby as though waiting their turn with the policemen. The officers recognized Mr. Newhouse and broke off their interview right away.

"Mr. Newhouse," one began, "we received complaints from your neighbors about a rowdy party here at the house. Loud music, hollering, and such. Upon investigation we found evidence of underage drinking and some marijuana use. We're taking statements now and will have a report filed in the morning. We tried contacting you at your place of business and by cell phone."

"I don't have a cell phone."

"Yes sir. We found that out. We need to know what kinds of charges you want to press, if any."

"I don't have no earthly idea right now," Newhouse replied and walked away from the officers to survey his invaded home. It looked like a war zone. In the den, furniture was overturned, lampshades removed to expose bulbs, cut glass snifters and shot glasses abandoned here and there. Disparate youths lingered in the den, waiting for something and regarding Mr. Newhouse as though *he* were the invader of their little bacchanal. He found the same scene in his dining and living rooms – upheaval of precious, costly items, evidence of his expensive alcohol being wasted. God knew what had been stolen. He said nothing to nobody, not even the young strangers who blocked his way as he went from room to room. For Winthrop Newhouse and his kind, the self-made man, silence was strength. A man let his actions speak for him, and so did a woman for that matter.

He sought out his grandson and found him where he had discovered him once before at about the same time of night – in his private study. The boy sat behind the vast oaken desk and smiled at his grandfather.

"Yo, dog. Come join the party. We even got the polices up in this hizzle."

"Shut your mouth. Shut your face. Just shut up, you ignorant-assed nothing. You disgrace. You wigger. Is that what you want to be? A wigger? Well congratulations." The boy spit out a laugh and kept laughing until the old man silenced him with a pounding fist on the door jamb. "I said shut up. You make me sick. This'll be in the newspaper. This'll be on TV. My name will be ruined. Everything I've worked for, for sixty years. Hell, I might end up in jail. I would have never dreamed that all my work would come to this...to you. They should have smothered you in your crib. They should have strangled you with the birth cord. No wonder your daddy left your mama. No wonder. He had the sense to get away from the likes of you. You're a shame. A nothing. A nastiness. The opposite of what I hoped for in a grandboy. I ought to send you out right now and make you sleep in the street. I ought to have them arrest you. But I'm too tired and too disgusted for anything."

With that Mr. Newhouse turned in the doorway and left Kyle Blackburn still sitting in the leather swivel chair.

Newhouse conferred briefly with the deputies. He would not press charges against any of the young men unless he found anything missing. He only wanted them out of his house as soon as possible. The officers assured him that no charges against him would be forthcoming, that it was obvious to them that he had not instigated the night's events. In a matter of half an hour, the Newhouse home was free of those who had ransacked it. Mr. Newhouse, exhausted in more ways than one, turned out only the den and dining room lights. He did not go back to the study. Clean-up and inventory would require help from Linda Bishop and would begin that next morning. It would also require that he do the unprecedented – take a non-vacation day off from Winner's Circle.

He returned to his bedroom and lay on the bed still in his work clothes, but he could not sleep and probably would not. His thoughts were troubled not so much by the breach of his property by these hooligans but by the face of his grandson as he had degraded him. He was so young, only fifteen, and, wigger or not, he was still a boy and of Newhouse blood. He looked so much like his mother, Newhouse's first born, with the hair blond and fine and the eyes brightly blue – and in turn Darlene, Kyle's mother, resembled to a T *her* mother, Newhouse's deceased wife. And he had wished the boy dead, right in front of him. Had called him a shame, a disgrace, a nothing. He was not the evil man as many in Compton had thought of him over the years. He was practical. He had worked and struggled for all he owned. He considered himself honorable, even if no one else did.

The boy would have to go back to Atlanta. That's all there was to it. He would call Darlene in the morning and demand she get to Compton as soon as possible to pick Kyle up. (That is if the police didn't come for him first. Goodness knew what their report would find.) Her heart had been in the right place, he reckoned, but not her head. She would have to do what she could to change the boy's behavior. But he did not want the departure to be marked by the ugliness of the evening. The least he could do would be to apologize to the boy for the harshness of his language and to offer him at least a sliver of hope.

He rose from his bed and went to the head of the stairs. From there, to his left, he could see that the study light still burned. He descended the stairs and went to the study. The boy still sat behind the desk. Newhouse opened his mouth to begin his apology when he realized his grandson held aloft and pointed at him one of Newhouse's prized Confederate pistols, an original Griswold and Gunnison made in Macon, Georgia.

"Boy, what in the world do you think you're doing?"

The boy's eyes narrowed to black slits. His gun hand tensed visibly.

"Haters has got to die, yo."

He squeezed the trigger. The long barrel exploded in a puff of blue smoke. Newhouse felt a shock of pain in his left arm which traveled up to his shoulder, spreading to his chest. His breathing grew shallow, weak. He stumbled backwards a couple of steps and fell, and everything around him plunged into darkness.

It turned out Mr. Newhouse was not injured by gunshot from his own collector's revolver. There was not even a bullet in the Griswold Gunnison. Gummed up gunpowder had caused the explosion. Mr. Newhouse had suffered a heart attack.

Both his daughters raced to Compton from their respective metropolises. They stood over their father, wired and tube-covered in his short bed but fully conscious. Darlene Blackburn, as always, assumed the role of spokeswoman.

"Kyle saved your life. Did you know that, Daddy? He called 911. Wasn't that smart of him? You might have died otherwise."

Mr. Newhouse spoke softly, carefully. "You be sure to thank him for me, won't you, hon?"

"Actually, he's right outside. You can thank him yourself."

Newhouse shook his head slowly. "You want me to get out of here sooner than later, don't you? Then don't bring that youngun in here."

Mrs. Blackburn's eyebrows flexed, nearly meeting each other. "What does that mean, Daddy? Are you saying...?"

"It's probably best if you get him back home as soon as possible. You got a lot of work to do on that boy."

"Daddy?"

"I'm not going to argue with you about this, Darlene. I'm going to be the daddy again, at least around here, for the time being, and give the orders. In case nobody's told you, I had a heart attack this morning. I can't imagine the doctor would recommend arguing for a man who's just had a heart attack. Can you?"

Mrs. Blackburn folded into herself. Her shoulders rose to meet her ears. He chin rose as well. Her arms became stiff at her sides. It was as though she were trying to will herself out of the hospital room without having to face further recriminations from her father. The other sister, the one who had come up from Charleston, as had always been her wont in the family, stood back and said nothing.

At a later visiting period Linda Bishop showed.

Mr. Newhouse smiled at her. "Take a look here," he said. "This is what you got to deal with."

Mrs. Bishop looked doubtful. "What you mean?"

Newhouse responded with mock offense. "I mean you got to look after me after they get me out of here and back home."

Mrs. Bishop snorted. "That what you think? Well, you got another thing coming, mister. I'm too young to take an old dog like you to raise."

The Dark Garden

I

Some people are just born assholes, you know? They just exit their mothers with assholism already installed or in the process of installation. History provides us a number of examples – Hitler, of course, everyone's favorite bungmunch, the Commie dictators, Mao, Pol Pot, etc. Literature too: think of Iago and all the jerks in Dickens and Captain Ahab and Holden Caulfield, whom I never could stand, the smart aleck closet case.

But plenty of local-grown assholes exist too, of course. And sometimes I wonder if I haven't had the displeasure of knowing most every one of them, right here in the South Carolina upcountry, at least those who lived and breathed in a certain time frame, oh, 1970 till the present day. I'm talking about Compton, South Carolina, which stands seventy miles north of Columbia and about the same distance southwest of Charlotte. It's a ghost of itself these days, with about thirty thousand residents and shrinking, but in olden times, when the cotton mills roared and hummed strong, it flourished and was one of the most promising little places in the southeast. Still, for its size, Compton has produced its fair share of hall-of-famer pricks: drunks, liars, cheats, braggarts, life-long bullies, and the like. To enumerate them all would take reams of paper and hours I don't really wish to spend on the topic. So I will take one for example: Darryl Pickett, who, by the way, is dead now, killed years ago at the very young age of thirty-seven when his truck went off the road and down an incline, throwing Darryl from his seat and breaking his neck. What I'm writing about occurred many years before that, in 1972, and culminated in one of the most bizarre episodes in the memory of just about anyone who was around then.

Darryl Pickett had some rightful claim to arrogance, I will admit. For one thing, he was two or three years older than most of the children who either lived on Byrd Street or spent much of their time there, as my sister and I did. Darryl lived with his mother in a kind of duplex apartment next door to our grandparents, Bert and Jesse McMillan, who tended to my sister and me in the summertime while our parents worked. Darryl's mother moved them there after his father died to be closer to her mother, Mrs. Sadie Gentry, who occupied an apartment in the same facility, as did Mrs. Gentry's older child, Ronnie, and his family, including his sons Fred and Sammy, with whom my sister and I played. They were, literally, a close, tight-knit family. Mrs. Gentry and my grandmother had grown up together and worked side by side as girls filling batteries in Compton Mill.

Darryl had the advantages too of being tall and good looking, with curling blond hair and sun-browned muscles. He could run fast and fight hard, and if he didn't win every fight he was purported to be in, he lied well enough to make us believe he had. He failed first grade twice, more out of laziness than lack of brains because goodness knows he could be cunning. He usually skipped school when he could manage it, to go smoke or fish or just to laze about in one of many hidden-away rural pockets in the county. His defiance in all things earned him respect from boys his own age and younger, and soon he had a gang of followers, a "posse," he called it, who roved about with him as he sought out mischief.

How specifically did he manifest his assholeness?

While I'd heard of him doing many things to many people younger than himself, I can really only speak in specifics from my own experience. I was an overweight child and therefore an ample mark for his taunts and name-calling. He gave us stingers, all of us, me, my sister, even his cousins Fred and Sammy, by repeatedly punching our tender younger arms with his stiff right middle knuckle until bruises emerged on the assaulted spots and remained there for days and were plenty painful. He swiped from us the candy and soft drinks we had procured from Mr. Fisher's general store just down the road from our grandmothers. He didn't eat or drink what he had taken from us but poured it on the ground or fed it to his dog, an old hound of indeterminate breed which he called Bronson after his favorite movie actor. He tripped us with his foot at every opportunity and once had my sister and me believing that our grandmother, Ninnie McMillan, had been mauled and killed by a grizzly bear which had gotten into the house. (Only Ninnie's sudden appearance on the front porch, bright, alive, and unmolested by animal or man, right in the middle of Darryl's vicious lie, quelled our hysterics.) Darryl's own grandmother, Mrs. Gentry, did not escape his hatefulness. He loved to send her in search of her missing dentures, up one side of the duplex and down the other, which he had removed while she sat asleep in her rocker on the porch, and it fazed him not one whit to frighten this old woman by leaving rubber spiders and snakes at various places in the house and even on her very person while again she slept unsuspecting. Often my sister and I, playing in Ninnie and Papa's dirt driveway, would hear Mrs. Gentry yell out next door at the discovery of such hideous objects, and there'd go Darryl scurrying away from the scene of the crime with his hand covering a giggle.

But all this was child's play in the context of greater assholery. Darryl Pickett's greatest masterwork of domestic terrorism, to crib some contemporary parlance, would be a thing of unimaginable depravity to the minds of pre-adolescents. It would involve a person heretofore unmentioned. And it would seal Darryl's own fate.

II

This unnamed individual was Otto Runnels. He and his family lived across the road from Ninnie and Papa McMillan in a two-story white-washed house up a sloping dirt road under the protection of an enormous locust tree. Mr. Runnels had met his wife while stationed in Germany in the early 1960s. Mrs. Runnels was a native of the country. By the early seventies, they were both heavyset and prematurely gray, looking more like grandparents than parents, and Mrs. Runnels'

English, despite a dozen years in America, remained a tangled thing, spoken in a sharp, metallic struggle with her native tongue.

Their sons, Ernest and Otto, both born in the States, were slim boys, Ernest tall and smiling and good-natured, Otto short, quiet, and reserved. In fact, Otto's silence was often mistaken by adults for reflection and meditation, even intelligence. Children our age, however, saw it as just one of his various idiosyncrasies. It was Darryl Pickett himself who early on dubbed the boy "Oddo" and "Oddball" and questioned aloud and to his face, whether he had been born in South Carolina as the Runnels claimed. Certainly his full mouth and tanned shading would not be found in the face and skin of just any Carolina boy. He had the look of a Mediterranean. And he had a strong preference for loneliness. His brother Ernest often reported to us that Otto talked to himself or to someone else he had imagined and that there were times he had caught Otto in strange forms of play in the backyard where he ran himself in circles and reached up to swat at his head from time to time as though he were being harassed by bees. He and I were not exactly close or steadfast friends, but I more than anyone else probably communicated to him on something more than just a superficial level (other than his family, that is). We shared an interest in comic books – what the old folks called "funny books" – and maintained a friendly rivalry on the quality of the leading houses: I was a DC partisan, he preferred Marvel. But we also collected and exchanged titles from more obscure publishers at the time such as Charlton Comics, which brought out *Captain Atom* and *Flash Gordon* in the nineteen-sixties, and Gold Key and King, whose covers were more garish, even more lurid, than those of the Big Two.

"Oddo," Darryl Pickett responded with sneering contempt. Ernest laughed. He was too friendly and trusting to realize he had just done his younger brother a world of harm by reporting his idiosyncrasies in front of Darryl.

III

Darryl and his sycophants had no use for Otto Runnels, but the rest of us tolerated him well enough, mainly because we liked his brother Ernest so very much. Ernest, around Darryl's age and even taller and bigger, was like an older brother to us. He rode us on his shoulders and chased blacksnakes from the road and back into the grass and defended us when Darryl became too aggressive, although they never fought each other. Ernest was a gentle giant. He probably could have hurt someone badly if he wished. Later, when I read John Steinbeck, he put me in mind of Lenny.

Because of Ernest, we let Otto run around with us when he chose to come down off the hill and play. He rarely said anything though, as was his nature. He surprised us with how well he rode my papa's pale stallion John. When he did speak, he could often say some very interesting things about flowers and trees and bugs. He could put names to things in Papa McMillan's backyard, although we had no way of knowing how accurate he was being.

Once Fred Gentry was bold enough to say, "Ernest says you talk a lot to yourself. That true?"

Otto shook his head slowly.

"Then who you talking to?"

Otto hesitated before he answered. "The sky. The sun. The sunflower. The worms in the ground. Everything."

No one responded to that until my sister wrinkled her nose and said, "Darryl Pickett's right. You are a durned old weirdo."

(My sister nursed a secret crush on Darryl Picket, whom she thought "cute," despite his harassing her.)

Once the lot of us, me, my sister, Fred, and Sammy, ventured up the hill to the Runnels residence. We found Otto with a short spade in his hand, working away at a certain section of the earth. When we asked him what he was digging for, he said, "China. I hear there are treasures galore there and lots of delicious tea too." We had heard the same thing but had never thought to go actually hunting for it from the remote grounds of Compton, South Carolina.

The central event of this recollection – the first of two actually – occurred the summer of 1972. It was a warm day in July. My sister and I were staying with Ninnie and Papa McMillan, while Daddy worked at Premier Designs, a new textile firm in Compton, and Mother for Mr. Barry Whitley, a former South Carolina state senator who had resumed his private law practice in town after quitting Columbia. It was not hot enough to prohibit outdoor gamboling, so our little gang collected on Byrd Street to play freeze-tag and hopscotch and sundry other diversions. Sometimes we were satisfied merely to forage among the honeysuckle vines massed along the roadside. We loved to draw out the thin chords from the blossoms and lick off the bit of nectar at the end. Otto Runnels was with us that day. So were our cousins Tina and Debbie Jean Montgomery, but they didn't stay with us very long. Debbie Jean was older than any of the rest of us, sixteen, and much more interested in movie magazines and talking on the telephone with her friends than in childish games, and when she abandoned us, she took Tina with her.

We were having a grand enough time when out of nowhere Darryl Pickett showed with a pair of his henchmen tagging along, Tommy Ireland and Scottie Jarman. Scottie lived with his family in a house to the left of Ninnie and Papa's. He was generally a good boy, unlike most Jarmans, so we could never understand his devotion to Darryl. Tommy was white trash from Broadusville, who illegally drove his Daddy's pick-up to Compton whenever he could. It was no wonder at all that he and Darryl hit it off. They were snakes from the same nest, so to speak.

Had they wanted, Darryl and Scottie and Tommy could easily have by-passed us and gotten to Scottie's house by cutting through Ninnie and Papa's front or back yard. But no: Darryl wasn't about to forgo a chance for a little mayhem. Meanness fed him along with blood and oxygen. So he and Tommy and Scottie strutted up Byrd Street, and Darryl made sure to name-call and thump ears and name-call some more. When he saw the hopscotch pattern Debbie Jean had drawn with pink chalk before her departure, he threatened to take out his tallywhacker and urinate it into non-existence. The three of them laughed their way through the Jarmans' front door. We went back to our play, smarting some from the physical and personal assault perpetrated by Darryl Pickett. After a while my sister left us to go find Tina and Debbie Jean. Not long after that, Sammy cried, "Look!" and pointed to my grandparents' house.

"What is it?" Fred asked his brother.

"More boys!" Sammy said. He was the youngest of all of us, perpetually dirty-faced from too much chocolate ice cream and scrape-kneed from being knocked to the ground too much by Darryl Pickett.

"Where? How many?"

"Behind yonder. I don't know how many. Maybe a hundred."

"Ain't no hundred boys behind Will's nanny's house."

"A'ight t'en. Maybe two hundred."

"Four," Otto said. He'd been pretty much quiet up to then. "There were four. I saw their shadows. They've gone into the Jarmans' backyard."

"Wonder what for?"

"I don't know. Want to go see?"

"I don't know."

"Maybe they going to pick a fight with Darryl and Tommy. Maybe they'll beat the tar out of Darryl."

"Only person I know can do that is Ernest Runnels. And he won't do it. Granny says he's too tender-hearted."

"It'd be worth seeing if it happens. Let's go."

So we went. Left that narrow portion of Byrd Street and trudged to Ninnie and Papa's backyard under the pretense of feeding green apples from the adjacent apple tree to John and his "wife," the sorrel mare Mary. We were disappointed to discover nobody in the Jarman backyard. Not a soul.

"W'ere'd they go?" Fred asked.

"Maybe they done killed each other and gone to heaven," Sammy offered.

"Ain't a one of them going to heaven," Fred answered. "Maybe Scottie. If he prays hard enough to Jesus to forgive him for hanging around Darryl and Tommy."

"They're in the barn," Otto said. He sighed. He had probably tired of this investigation and wanted actually to feed John and saddle him up for a ride. He had such a natural look when he rode, as though he'd been born on the back of a stallion.

Like my Papa McMillan, Ed Jarman had constructed a wood structure behind his house. Papa used his to store baled hay and sundry outdoor implements. We didn't know what resided in Mr. Jarman's because we'd never been in it. At least I hadn't.

"How do you know, Otto?" I asked.

"I can see their eyes shine through the slats of the barn."

"Really?"

He didn't answer that except to say, "Seven pairs of eyes."

"Wonder what they doing in yonder?"

"Probably smoking cigarettes. Or looking at dirty pictures."

"Dirty pictures? Of nekkid girls?"

"What else, dumb-dumb?"

"Ah-woo!"

The Dark Garden

Otto's obvious boredom at all this only increased, and he began to meander over to the pen where John lolled his enormous head on the fence, no doubt yearning for those green apples our presence had promised him. We followed Otto, apples in hand, and were so busy feeding the horse and, forgive the pun, horsing with each other, we did not hear the mash of grass and rock underfoot, were not aware of the four boys behind us, until they caught our shoulders and yanked us toward them and began to move us, away from the fence, out of my grandparents' yard, into the Jarmans', across the ground, and into Mr. Jarman's shed upon which the heavy wooden doors were closed on us and we were left in a semi-darkness lit only by the summer sun slicing through crevices in the shed's woodwork. Thus blinded, even partially, our sense of smell sharpened, and we were assaulted by a hybrid tang of metal, oil, and resin that joined fear and bewilderment in nearly choking us.

"Darryl!" Fred Gentry hollered. "I know it's you."

"'Cause you so damn smart," Darryl answered glumly, only a voice at the moment and not a face or figure.

"Let us go! We ain't done nothing to you."

"Will when we get ready."

And I thought I heard the sound of fist on flesh, followed by Fred's grunt.

"We ain't got no money."

"Who says we want it?"

"Then what do you want, son of a bitch?"

Another thud, another groan.

"We'll holler."

"We'll break your arm too, you nasty-mouthed little bastard. I'm going to tell Granny Gentry what a nasty mouth you got."

"Go ahead. Granny Gentry thinks you a son of a bitch too. Just ask her. Ow! Quit it!"

"Shut your smart mouth, Fred."

"All you got to do is bother other people. Some kind of life you got, Darryl Pickett."

This was Otto Runnels, shocking everybody in the shed by speaking.

"Oddo," Darryl mocked. "I'm surprised you ain't some place digging up the ground. What in the hell is it, Oddo, you digging for?"

"A world you don't live in."

"Freak of nature. How come it is a freak of nature like you keeps alive?"

It was a cryptic question, and Otto delivered a cryptic response.

"By not being you."

It sounded as though Darryl hissed. Afterwards he said, "Tommy, take holt of Fred here. I got to prepare my surprise for Oddo."

There was a shift of movement in the shed, a shuffling, more grunts, the hard sound of gripping.

"What sort of surprise?" Fred, not Otto, asked.

"Wouldn't be no surprise if I told."

Tommy Ireland laughed.

"You sure you can do it, Darryl?" And he laughed again.

"Hell yeah," Darryl answered from the deepest shadows of the shed. "Been eating prunes. All day. Drinking castor oil. Even took me a Ex-Lax. I'm 'bout ready to blow up, boys!"

That pronouncement cleared all noise in the shed, but the silence was soon assaulted by the noise of flatulence of modulating decibels, the initial farts small, timid, quick, the later ones brash, shameless, atomic, and rushing in behind them was the unmistakable odor of – well, Fred Gentry, who at nine had somewhere, somehow taken an advanced course in obscenity, put it best –

"Shit," he said innocently. "Darryl, what you doing? Taking a shit back yonder?"

The confines of the shed, mixed with human sweat and plain fear and uncertainty, as well as Darryl's emerging feces, got a fierce grip on my guts and punched up to my throat again and again. I gagged gently at first, then harder, audibly.

"Hey!" the boy holding me whispered. (I never figured out who he was.) "Don't you vomit on me!" And he let me go. I took the moment to dash, to make my get away, and nobody tried to stop me.

I squeezed through the doors of the shed and ran, out of the Jarman yard, back into my Ninnie and Papa's. The retch had been arrested in my throat and hung there and hurt, as though a knife were being gouged into my esophagus. I wish I could have thrown up. I leaned against the side of my grandparents' house and let the clear air dissolve the vomitus knot – the good smells of ripe green apples, cut grass, and sunshine. I looked behind me to see if anyone from Darryl's gang had followed me. No. I hated to leave Fred and Sammy and Otto in their clutches. I felt like such a coward but could not go back and try to rescue them. There was evil in that little wooden building, everything I'd been warned about at home and church and school. So I scrambled into the house and buried myself in a summer-warmed room until Mama came for Lisa and me.

IV

"It's about the worst thing I ever seen," Fred Gentry told me the next day. He wasn't mad at me for running from Darryl and Tommy and the others.

"I don't blame you," he said. "I'd've run myself if I could have. Sammy ain't mad neither. But I don't know about Otto. I ain't talked to him since yesterday."

Otto.

Darryl had been making a "surprise" for Otto when I got away.

What had it been?

"Will, I didn't know folks could go so low down like Darryl Pickett went yesterday. I'm beginning to wonder if Darryl ain't gone and lost his mind or done got possessed by the devil."

"What happened?"

"You really want to know?"

"Yes. I guess so."

With that permission, Fred related what happened in the shed after I had escaped it. As the details unfolded, I couldn't help but wonder if Fred were making things up just for the sake of sensationalism. But he told everything with a straight face, never betraying a lie or a fabrication.

"Shit," he said, not swearing but naming the fact of the matter or the matter of the fact or the matter of the fart.

"You know what Darryl done back yonder in the dark?"

"How could I, Fred. I ran away."

"He took a shit on a paper plate. He'd been messing with his belly all day to make a number two. And boy he done it. A number two, three, and four from the way it smelled."

"How did you stand it, Fred? Why didn't you run too?"

"Darryl brought it to us, his own shit on that plate, like it was something good to eat."

"I want to puke just thinking about it."

" – and said, 'Who wants it? Who wants it?' Making them other boys laugh their heads off. But he only meant me and Sammy and Otto. Of course nobody wanted it. But it was Otto's 'surprise.' He said that at the beginning. Don't know why he was offering it to anybody else. And he went over to Otto with the plate balanced in the palm of his hand and held it to Otto's face. Run it back and forth under his nose. Then said, 'This ort to keep that mouth of yours too busy to smart off to anybody. And then he –"

"No, Fred, no! You can't mean it!"

" – right in his face. Mushed it real good in Otto's face. Took the plate off and – "

"Didn't Otto fight? Didn't he say nothing?"

" – it left this mask of dookie all over his face. Chunks of it fell so you could see his eyes and mouth underneath."

"Didn't Otto say anything, Fred? Anything at all?"

"Not a word."

V

"I think you done made your point, Darryl," Scottie Jarman had said with a laugh. Somewhere he found a cloth rag and offered it to Otto to clean his face. Otto refused it. Now released by the boy holding him, he instead turned and pushed open the doors of the shed and walked out. He didn't run or sprint. He went slowly, calmly, as though he'd been the head of a pre-adolescent tribunal which had just concluded its business. Fred even used the word "dignified" to describe the way Otto made his exit.

No one had followed him. Subsequently there had been no visiting by parents over the incident, no summoning of the law to investigate and arbitrate. It was as though it had been normal child's play or had never happened at all or as though Otto had taken no offense whatsoever at having his face smeared with another boy's excrement. He never spoke a word about it, just went about things in his usual Otto Runnels way – digging his holes to nowhere, cavorting with phantoms, communing with the natural world in his own quixotic fashion.

Little did we know Otto was merely biding his time, waiting for the right moment, the right circumstance to repay Darryl Pickett for his unspeakable offense.

VI

I got bits and snatches of what happened over the next few weeks, of how Darryl Pickett disappeared one afternoon, was gone overnight, and had been discovered the next day, not very far from his house, in unplanted ground adjacent to City View Cemetery, buried up to his neck in a six-foot hole, packed to incapacitation by black soil and by wounds to his arms and legs and head...all courtesy of Otto Runnels.

I received the complete narrative from Otto himself, not long before he left Compton for the psychiatric hospital in Greenville, where he would spend two years before returning home, at which time he would navigate his life up to now in even more bizarre terms than those of his childhood.

"Sometimes the worm needs to be put back in the ground," he started. We were sitting on the front porch of his family's house in the waning days of summer vacation. It was just him and me.

"How did you do it?" I asked. "How did you get Darryl out yonder?"

"You can talk stupid people into almost anything."

"Are you some sort of genius, Otto? You talk like a grown-up, not a ten-year-old."

He didn't answer the question. He looked off into the summer sky and began telling.

He had merely walked up to Darryl on Darryl's front porch in the middle of the day.

"You got to come with me, Darryl," he had begun simply.

Darryl had laughed before his mouth settled into a steady sneer.

"What the hell you talking about, Oddo? What the hell you want?"

"You got to come with me, Darryl. You got to see it for yourself."

"Do what?"

"You got to see it!"

"What?"

"At the cemetery. Somebody's dug it up. A big place in the earth. And it's laying there, Darryl."

"What is?"

"The corpse. The body. Still in its clothes. Somebody has dug it up. For whatever reason. Can't tell if it's white or black or Indian or what."

Darryl had snorted.

"If it's in City View, it's white. That's all they let in City View. They don't put in black or Indian. Don't you know nothing, Oddo?"

"I reckon you're right, Darryl, but...I don't know. It's not exactly in the cemetery. It's kind of outside it. Away from it some. In a wilder spot of ground. That's what makes it so strange, you know. It's like a secret grave outside the graveyard. Like who was buried wasn't good enough for City View or was too different or bad or something and had to settle for exile."

Darryl had at first remained unimpressed, but Otto could espy some evidence of growing interest in the muscles of his jaw and face and in a faint glint in his eyes. Maybe he was merely pondering what the hell *exile* meant.

"What the hell, Oddo? What do you want? If I go with you to see this thing, will you leave me the hell alone?"

It was, as I said, not a very long trek to the object of Otto's perfervid fascination. They went behind the Gentry/Pickett duplex, cut across part of Ninnie and Papa McMillan's backyard, and plunged into a mass of blackberry bramble, polk salad fronds, poison oak, and dandelion stalks. They crossed a dried-up bottom rich with flint that divided private property from public and skirted the outermost grounds of City View Cemetery. They moved right from there and entered a brief woods made up exclusively of pines and black soil.

"If you made this up, Oddo, just to walk me the hell to death...."

But no. Otto pointed. "Right here. Up just a way." And there it was, under a rectangle of sunlight – the hole, of the regular depth for burying a body the civilized way, six feet or thereabouts. Maybe a bit less. They walked up close to the hole together and looked about.

"You said they was a body," Darryl said standing still and looking around him, as though a body very much alive might come walking their way from City View. "Where is it?"

"It was here. Right here," Otto replied innocently, plaintively. He left Darryl's side and walked towards the mounds of dirt which dressed this make-shift grave on all four sides and roved around the gap, peering into it. All of a sudden he began leaping about like a scalded chimpanzee. He pointed into the hole. "There!" he said. "There it is!"

Darryl eyed him suspiciously, doubtfully. "You mean to tell me that dead body got up and crawled back into its grave? Otto, are you shitting me, son?"

"I'm telling you that body's right there. Come look!"

Darryl strode over, skeptical, and looked into the grave. He saw nothing else but sheer black soil on all four walls of the hole, with mere hints of green grass sprouting here and there. He didn't see a body.

"Otto!"

And he didn't see Otto take the red-pan shovel from its resting place behind the pine tree, the one Otto had used to dig the hole himself. But he did, of course, feel the shovel's whack against his right kneecap, felt it so acutely that he bowed at the grave's edge, as though offering the invisible dead some reverence. Otto wasted no time in lifting his weapon again and again, delivering blows to Darryl's shoulder, his back, and finally his head. With that last whack, Darry toppled gently, delicately into the hole. He *became* the body in the grave, although he was still living. With the speed available only to the energized young, Otto began shoveling the dirt back into the gap from which he'd dug it so many hours before, taking no time to enjoy the plosh of black grit on Darryl's unconscious face. It was the face only left visible after Otto had packed the ground back into place. The rest of Darryl had vanished. His work done, Otto returned the shovel to its place against the tree and took a seat a half dozen feet from where Darryl's head protruded from the earth like some gruesome, exotic fungus, an enormous mushroom equipped with eyes and mouth and nose and blood-knotted blond hair. He was determined to sit as long as it took to greet Darryl back to consciousness.

The day dimmed before that happened, before Darryl's eyelashes fluttered like moths' wings. His eyes eventually opened and stared ahead without recognition of the thin brown boy seated swami-like, legs crossed, before him, half-smiling.

"Hey, Darryl. You're not dead. That's good. I didn't want you to die. Not yet anyway. I wanted you to live and suffer. I want to make you suffer, so that if you do live, you'll never, ever shove a plate of your shit into anybody else's face again. You miserable son of a bitch. You scum of the earth. What I should do, I guess, is squat right over you and take a shit on your empty head, or a piss, or both, so you'll know just how it feels. But I'm not. I'm going to leave you here, by yourself, all night long, and hope to God a coyote comes along and eats your face slowly, bit by bit, or a copperhead crawls in your mouth or a hoot owl pecks out your eyeballs."

And he did just what he said he'd do. He stood and turned and left Darryl to the whims and mercies and unguessable perils of Mother Nature.

VI

It was early the next morning before Darryl Pickett was discovered and rescued. By then, of course, Darryl's mother, who loved and even idolized her son so much she'd become blind to his cruelty, had become frantic and had called everyone she could think of who might know something of Darryl's whereabouts. But it was gamboling children who found him, a pair of pre-adolescents, a boy and a girl, a brother and a sister, who did not run in our little circle of friends. They'd gone out early to do goodness knew what within the confines of City View. In their wandering of the grounds, they came upon Darryl's bodiless head as though finding a broken toy buried in the ground or the aforementioned *fleur de mal*. They circled it and prodded at it with fingers and sticks to test whether or not it still lived, and when Darryl, now fully conscious, hollered at them, "Cut out that foolishness and help me, damn it!" they jumped and squealed and ran home to tell their mother.

Ronnie Gentry, Fred and Sammy's daddy, and Fred and Sammy themselves were the ones who dug Darryl up and got him to Marshall Bates Hospital only a couple of miles northeast of the cemetery. The emergency room doctor found a severe concussion to the head, a broken kneecap, lacerations to the back and to the right arm, and dehydration. They admitted Darryl to the hospital and summoned someone from the sheriff's office. But Darryl refused to disclose the details of his abduction. He wouldn't say anything. He just stared ahead as though catatonic.

"He was ashamed," Fred Gentry told me later, "because it was Otto Runnels who got the best of him. And he did. Old Otto got Darryl real good."

And it was Otto who came forth to the authorities. He recalled to them the whole incident with more than just a hint of pride in his voice.

VII

The last time I saw Darryl Pickett was six years before he died in a one-vehicle car accident. For whatever reason, probably speeding, maybe drinking, he lost control of his truck and went into a steep embankment. He was thrown from the driver's seat and killed immediately by a broken neck. He was thirty-seven years old. He left behind a wife and two young children.

It was a late July afternoon when I last saw him and humid as all get-out. Fat black clouds promised a rancorous thunderstorm and kept good on that promise an hour later. I'd gone over to my folks to invite them in person to supper at an Italian restaurant which had just opened up several blocks east of downtown, the first of its kind in Compton. When I swung into their driveway, however, I found a red pick-up sitting behind Daddy's Fairmont and Mother's Taurus. Black lettering on the door read: PICKETT FLOORING AND UPHOLSTERY. I had no idea.

Daddy met me at the backdoor, casting a glance at the ominous sky.

"Be careful," he said. "We having some work done in here."

And sure enough when I entered the house and looked down at the den floor, I saw that its old hardwood had been completely obliterated and obscured by green-checkered linoleum tiles.

"The kitchen too," Daddy instructed me and led me there. (Mother, forever bashful of strangers, had retreated to her and Daddy's bedroom down the hall, probably to take a shameful cigarette break; smoking cigarettes was her great secret from the world, one we were all sworn never to reveal.) And there, crouched down smoothing more tiles of green linoleum were a young man and a boy just nearing adolescence or maybe a year or so beyond it. The man wore jeans and a red tee-shirt, and he had curling blond hair which he kept hidden beneath an old baseball cap and a golden moustache as thick as the mane of a woman's hairbrush. The boy was thin and gawky with short, flat brown hair.

Daddy looked at me, grinned, and pointed to the man.

"I bet you don't remember who this fella is, do you?" he asked.

I looked at the stranger and smiled at him and at Daddy. Then I shook my head.

"No sir I don't."

"This is Darryl Pickett. Remember Darryl? Growed up right next to Mama and Daddy down on Byrd Street. Missrus Gentry's grandboy. He's grown into a fine-looking young man."

All the while Darryl never stopped his work.

I studied him a moment and everything became clear. For a second his moustache vanished, leaving Darryl's handsome-hateful face beneath it, this time grinning shyly.

"I sure do remember him," I said at last. I held out my hand to him. He stood and took it, his eyes fastened to mine, glinting ambiguously. But I couldn't tell if they communicated a challenge as of old or a plea. I smiled deeply at him and said, "And I remember he was mean as the devil too. Used to give the rest of us boys and girls hell on Byrd Street."

Right away I saw the color, bloody red, rise from Darryl's neck into his face, blotting out his tan. And I started to add, "Till crazy old Otto Runnels put him in his place," but for some reason that struck me as gratuitous.

"Did he really?" Daddy asked, delighted.

I nodded. Daddy laughed. I laughed too. Darryl Pickett didn't laugh but returned to the floor and the job at hand.

Miss Blitch of Helton Avenue

Some people are born old. You know that? They come out of the cabbage patch gray-haired and whiskered, wrinkled, stooped, and hoarse-voiced.

That's how it was for Miss Ida Blitch of Helton Avenue.

The stork dropped her on her mama and daddy's front step all ready for the old folks' home.

If you don't believe me, go find an old Compton High School yearbook, The Compton High *Mirror*, and see for yourself. Go way back. Nineteen-fifty-something. Turn to the teacher section. There she is, Miss Blitch, hair turned in a long white wave, bosom and belly broad as that of an old woman who never took care of herself. How old was she *then*? Nobody knows. She wouldn't say. If you get a-hold of Moses or Methuselah, they might remember her. Otherwise, you're out of luck. But don't *ever* ask her yourself; she'll cuss you out black and blue.

(By the way, if you find that copy of *The Mirror* or even a copy she's not in, for goodness sake, don't show it to her. She hated the yearbook. Know why? No one ever dedicated one to her. Ever. Not in the forty-something years she taught English at Compton High School did one yearbook editor dedicate *The Mirror* to her. On the day in late spring when they handed them out, she'd get hold of a copy and run it down from cover to cover, from copy to advertisements, right in front of the poor young'uns who had spent all year putting it together. That's how hateful she was.)

The boys at school showed what they thought of her. "Blitch the Bitch!" they said on the Compton High grounds and in the lunch room. Sometimes they whispered it in the classroom with her there sitting in her desk. One boy would begin with "Blitch" and another would finish up with "the Bitch?" Of course the young'uns heard it and laughed. She heard it too, and that's when class would be done for the day. She spent the rest of the time giving them a Sunday school-type lesson on the wickedness of the wrong words. Then she would let them go, saying she would pray for whoever would say such an awful thing.

Blitch the Bitch!

Where did she come from? How did she get here? Outer space? Who knows? She was just here, always had been and remains so. And how old? A hundred? Two hundred? A thousand years old? Your guess is as good as mine. She was just one of those old-lady school teachers who crowd a little place like kudzu. There's no getting rid of them.

A husband? Children? Good Lord no! Who'd have her? Who'd *she* have, Miss Ida Blitch, turning her nose up at the school yearbook and making those poor children go away from her classroom feeling like dirt?

"But she's got a pretty face," some would say of her, trying to find something redeeming. And true. Her face was small like a doll's with a little red bow mouth. But the tongue! The tongue that came out of that face with a viper's hatefulness and hurt! It ruined any effect the rest of her face might have had.

Actually, she is said to have had a fiancé once. Or a boyfriend. Or something. She said it. But nobody else saw him. She said he came to her house on Helton Avenue in what used to be the Mill Village in Compton and take her out. He was from out of town and very nice-looking. *She said.* And said they went to the Perry Cinema downtown to watch *Ben-Hur* with Charlton Heston. Then they had a nice meal at the Corsage Room in the old Excelsior Hotel (now no longer there). But nobody else saw all that coming and going. Until.... until...some folks got the idea for a good joke and said they *had* seen it, and they saw Miss Blitch and her beau return to the house on Helton Avenue. Some said he left way late at night out the back door. Others said he didn't leave at all and wondered what happened to him. "She killed him and cut him up and put him underneath her floor piece by piece!" one storyteller had it, like the crazy fellow in that story we read in school. Now how could she have done all that, with her sister, Miss Ila Blitch, a better, much nicer person, living right there in the same house and not saying a word? Some took their little game even farther and said Miss Ida and Miss Ila ganged up on this fellow and loved him to death then took him out and buried him in the backyard!

No.

People talk too much about things they don't know a thing about.

All I know is, this Johnny Spitshine, real or not, never married Ida Blitch, and neither did anybody else. And that she lives there still on Helton Avenue, Miss Ila gone now for years, looked after by nieces and nephews and must be coming up on...what?...a hundred years old by now? Or a million? I don't know.

I just wonder in the first place why anybody bothers about what happens to an old maid.

Crow Boy

This story is for Ben Greer, fellow upcountryman

The South Carolina Upcountry: 1955

He hears them talking through the swinging door.

"Now what are you crying for? He's the same. Everything's the same, I tell you."

"I know but I can't help but worry."

"About what? He's the same and as healthy as can be expected."

"You're a man, Dr. Randall. These things don't affect men the way they do women. The constant worrying over the least thing. That's a woman's lot in life. You ought to know that by now with all the women you've talked to through the years."

"He's healthy as a horse. He eats well. He sleeps well. His blood and heart rate are normal."

There is silence.

"Now I told you – it's a mental condition, not a physical one. He's not an idiot by any means. Just slow with a tendency to keep to himself."

"I can't help but believe he's being cheated out of something, and I want to give it back to him – so badly! And would if I could! I'd give up my whole life!"

A sob, then silence.

"You're the one who decided against psychiatric evaluation."

"If we were living in a big town it would be different."

"Well then."

The door opens some and the woman, his mama, comes through first. She stands in the door a moment, her face all red and wet, but she is smiling and very pretty in her blue dress and white hat with the flowers banked on the brim. And then the man appears behind her who pushes his mama on through the door gently with two fingers and follows her. The man is white-haired and wears glasses and a wide smile. They both smile at him but he does not smile back. He sits on the examining table spread with plastic, his shirt off, and is staring once again at the thing he wanted to see most ever since they left him alone to go into the hall and talk: it hangs around the man's neck by a split rubber chord and looks like a thimble, except it's silver and cold. The man would not let him touch it but he touched him with it. Here. There. Leaving the cold on his skin a moment. "Ticker sounds good," the man had told him and moved the thimble to his back. Now the man is smiling and coming towards him, and the thimble is low on his neck, almost ready to drop. It flares in a ray of sunshine through the slat-split window as though trying to speak to him, to communicate in a language all its own. He doesn't want it to drop.

"You been a fine young man today," the man says smiling and getting closer to him. The thimble moves and shines in its language of light, telling him something, communicating some desire to him. "Wish all boys were like you." But he does not feel so good now. He is worried now what might happen should the thimble hit the floor.

Would it disappear for good? It is so low on the man's neck, near his bellybutton, and slipping further. Doesn't the man know? When the man gets close enough, talking and smiling, when he stands just outside the v-crack of his spread legs, he reaches out and snatches it with both his hands to keep it from falling – to save the bit of sun in it.

"Hey, hey! What's the matter there?" The man takes it back from him. "You've been after my stethoscope ever since you got here. You may hold it but you must give it back."

It shines too good to drop.

In the car he sits in the backseat pressed against the door. His mama has told him never to sit like that, that the door might open and he might be lost to the road. But he sits pressed against the door anyway. His mother looks back at him through the white veil she has drawn over her face against the sun and kept drawn even in the car – to hide her tears. "Sugar. I have told you not to lean so hard on the door. You might fall out! Here. You want another cracker? I've got another cracker in my purse. Will that make you sit up straight? Here. Sit up and eat the cracker. Maddie will be a long time with supper yet."

Big Black Man is driving. He looks in the mirror at him and smiles. "I wish my mamie was here to feed me crackers! Lawd if I don't!"

He laughs. "Big Black Man ain't got no mama!"

"Now here!" his mama says. "What have I told you about calling him that? His name is Charles. You are to call him Charles. And of course he has a mother. How do you think he got here?"

"Big Black Cow had him! That's what Daddy says!" He twists himself up with his laughter. His shoulders nearly meet and his head disappears between them and his legs cross.

"Now here! Eat your crackers and hush such talk as that." His mama's veil is up and her face is red. She is red, white, and blue today.

He leans back against the door and sniffs the cheese between the saltines. "No sir. I ain't no idiot. I'm a Flowers. Russell Bankhead Flowers II. Route Two. Beaslap, South Carolina. Mama says to tell them that if you get lost. So I say I'm Russell Bankhead Flowers II Route Two, Beaslap, South Carolina, and that will get me back home. My daddy is not from Beaslap. He stays in Columbia and talks about roads all day long. The Road. The One Compton County Must Have If It is To See Itself Into the Twenty-First Century and Beyond." His daddy says that in Columbia, and in Beaslap, and in Compton, whenever he is here.

"Mama, how come Daddy talks about roads all day long?" he asks, cheese and cracker tumbling from his lips.

"Because Daddy wants a good road to come through Compton and make everybody happy."

"Big Black Man? Would a good road make you happy?"

"Rusty, I thought I told you –"

"Would it?"

"I reckon it would, Rusty. Reckon it'd make me happy as a hog in mud."

At home his mama makes him wash his hands in the kitchen sink. Then she goes into his room to pick out his summer clothes. She still wears the veil over her face.

"Come and change, Rusty. You cannot stay in those good town clothes. Rusty, come and change, and Mama will let you read the funny papers. You want to read the Katzenjammer Kids? You can read it to Mama. She'll tell your teacher how well you can read. Rusty! Charles, would you please bring him in here? Now, Rusty, don't fight Charles. This is not a joke. This is not fun. You cannot stay in those good clothes."

Later, when he is in his room, changed from his town clothes to his summer clothes, he sprawls on the floor with the funny papers. He reads Dick Tracy, not the Katzenjammer Kids. He likes Gravel Gertie. Gravel Gertie has a bald spot on the top of her head and keeps a gun under her dress. He reads every word very slowly. Miss Gatlin at the school says to say every word very slowly to yourself like it's a big piece of gum and you are chewing it over very carefully and that the longer you say the word and chew it up, the longer that word will stay with you. It will stick to you like gum. Miss Gatlin waits for him outside everyday at the school in Spartanburg. She is small and nervous and pretty and very kind. She waits at the front gate, and when Big Black Man pulls up, she opens the car door and says, "Why, lands, I believe we've got us a learning man here! A scholar of the English language!" He did not go to school today for he had to let the man poke him with the thimble, and as much as he likes Miss Gatlin and her soft voice and warm hands, he does not like school as much as the coming to and going from school because it is then his mother is not in the car and he can sit in the front seat with Big Black Man. Big Black Man wears a grey coat with big brass buttons down the front, and when the sun falls on them, the buttons burn like yellow fire. Big Black Man gets mad when he reaches over and yanks at the buttons.

"He-yah," he says in his coal-black voice. "What do you mean by such, Mr. Man? Do you think just 'cause your daddy's the senator he can afford to buy me a new livery every time you take a notion for a brass button?"

"It shines good."

"So will your eye mister if you do not keep your hands to yourself."

Gravel Gertie has a big fat gun stuck against Dick Tracy's head. "You can-not un-der-es-ti-mate a wo-man," she tells him and he chews the words aloud so they stick. He lays his head on the paper, as though reading the one sentence has exhausted him. His head feels so heavy now. The funny paper is warm and the smell of the ink is thick and chokes him some. He turns over on his back to escape it. He wants to sleep. He wants to go to sleep and dream. Of the golden calf. Mama reads to him about it in the Bible stories. "And they raised an idol...a golden calf, in defiance of the Lord...." she starts, and ends, "The Lord struck it down with his mighty lightning! See there, Rusty. If you defy the Lord...." He knows. He knows all that. Miss Gatlin has told him. The Sunday school teacher has told him. He wants to see the calf hit by lightning. No, he wants to see it hit by sunlight. He wants to see them raise it to the sun and the sun fall down on it and make it shine. He wants that golden *brilliance*, as Miss Gatlin might say in her soft, kind voice that suddenly rises with the excitement of a new and more *complicated* word. He wants the golden calf so bad now he can almost see it in the yellow paint on his ceiling. Oh God, don't strike it down with lightning. It shines too good.

"Rusty, get up off that floor. Do you want a bug to crawl in your ear? Get on the bed if you're going to sleep."

He stands. "No ma'am, I don't want no inseck in my ear."

She turns and leaves. She will go and take her own afternoon nap before supper. Big Black Man and Maddie and the others will play cards in Charles's room behind the main house and sip cooking sherry and laugh and talk about when they were young. They might even put on records and dance and sing to them. He has been there and seen them do it and even tried a little of the sherry himself. He has never danced however.

It is the only time he has, while the sun is still high in the sky, and he must go *now*, before Mama wakes and misses him.

Outside, he lifts his legs high like a racehorse's. He loves to hear his feet stamp on the ground. He is happy now, as he always is at the beginning of these trips. The air comes into his lungs sharp as a knife and makes him feel that if he can breathe enough of it, he will lift right off the ground and float to where he needs to go. He's a man on his own. No, mama, no daddy, no Big Black Man.

"It's mine," he says to himself then says it out loud. "It don't belong to no other soul but me. Not Daddy, not Mama, not Big Black Man, nor Maddie, nor Sadie Mae, not even Miss Gatlin, nice as she is." He walks forward, staring ahead into the woods, hoping its doors, its windows, its crooked roof, will come into view soon, but it's a long ways off and he keeps marching like a soldier. He stamps past the old Beaslap Yarn Mill with its broken windows and garlands of kudzu. "I ain't coming to see *you!*" he tells it and leaves it like a child rejected and goes on.

He found it, this house, last Christmas, when he had run out of his Mama and Daddy's house, no matter what his mama said about Jack Frost, to find a real Christmas tree and not a plastic one. It was high in the day, the sun cold as an ice cube, and he just kept running, like some crazy horse, couldn't stop himself, and the trees ran past him and the roads cut away everywhere – he forgot about finding the Christmas tree, all of a sudden it didn't matter anymore – and he felt he could run till the Kingdom Come, though he didn't know where he was or where he would end up, but then he saw it – the tip of its roof came up out of a patch of little trees, and he stopped then, breath gone and his feet still wanting to move. *It* stopped him, the crooked roof with the chimney about to fall over. He went to it, got on his hands and knees and crawled through the short tunnel of brush and limbs till he came to it, the little house of unpainted and splintery wood, leaning to one side, like it was listening to somebody talking. The porch was gone, the windows blinded with ruined and slashed paper shades. "It's mine," he said then, out loud, and breathed hard. "It must be mine. It made me stop running, didn't it? It peeked out from the trees and stopped me and drew me close to it." He went in. The house was a blot of night in the bright winter day. It took him a while before his eyes could make out the piles of planks and broken glass, the tattered wall paper, the broken limbs of chairs and tables, the gaps in wall and floor. And the pot-bellied stove. Sitting there in what was once the kitchen, all alone, in shadows, like a runaway itself, a refugee. He had turned and started his crazy run back home, all excited, but he went back to the little house everyday that week, near dark, to see if any light burned in the broken windows. Then one morning, as everybody else slept, he took the duffel bag his daddy had given him when he turned thirteen from under his bed. It was heavy with everything, all he owned, and he took it and ran to the place, which he also owned now, ran as hard as he could, holding the bag close to his chest. It rattled. It shook. It wanted to take him down to the ground. Oh he couldn't wait to see everything shine there in that dark place.

"It's mine," he says now, aloud, so many months later. He has marked it with the duffel bag in the belly of the black stove. That makes it his.

He marches ahead now, and now is when he begins to feel sad. The house will not come into sight. The trees keep coming, green and fat and full, and the little dirt roads whip around him like the paths in a maze. It saddens him too that he has nothing new to bring to his duffel bag. He would have liked the doctor's thimble – what does *he* need it for? It was hanging off his neck – but the doctor flung it over his shoulder so he could not reach for it again.

He's sad now, and his head is heavy with the sad. He slows down and wants to go to the red dirt road and weep. "I hate you house!" he says aloud. He is sure the house has gotten up and moved just to spite him. And it is then, just when he least expects it and has almost given up on finding the house, that he sees a familiar pattern, the sad, slender clutch of trees, no taller than a man, with the sad sagging roof more on top of the trees than behind them, and it is then he throws himself into a run, knocking aside branches. He comes up, out of the storm of twigs and limbs and thorns, out into the high bright sun again, where it stands before him, the house, not making any fuss at all that he has returned, just standing there unmoved and unsurprised.

He goes to the house, to its front door barely hanging from its hinges, and reaches out to hook his index finger into the splintery hole where the doorknob once was, but he stops right away and pulls backs, draws back from the house, as though it has struck out at him with a splintery hand. Something is not right. It is not his anymore. It has another smell to it, a sharp skunk smell, and not the smell it had when he first came upon it and returned to it again and again, the smell of old and unpainted wood, the smell of gas, of hunting mice. He goes back to the house, cautious now and sad too. He steps in but doesn't want to. It's got another smell. He walks forward a little, sees the upturned chair and table, sees the pot-bellied stove like a gnome huddled in the day-lit darkness, and turns, turns so fast and hard he sends a loose plank in the floor flying and crashing. A storm of dust. "It ain't mine no more."

"Who the hell's in here? Who is that?" It's a Big Man's voice like his daddy's. It makes him stop, automatically, as his own daddy's does. He does not want to stop, but it's a deep voice, it's got the sound of law in it, and he does. He turns and sees them, two Big Men, tall and lean, coming out of the long shadow in the back of the room. Two of them, one behind the other, and they're smiling.

"I thought it was mine," he says, looking down at the floor.

"Thought what was yours?"

They are Big Men, both, but not so big as his daddy or Big Black Man. One has black hair above his lip, the other is smooth-faced. One is dark-headed, the other light. One is taller than the other one. They are the both of them shirtless, and their pale knotted smooth muscles light up that corner of the room. They smile, and there is something bright and dreamy and far away in their eyes. He can tell that, even in the deep dusk of the room. One of them holds a tiny cigarette and puffs deeply off it before handing it to the other. "What's your name, man?"

"Russell Bankhead Flowers the Second, Route Two, Beaslap, South Carolina."

"You that senator's boy?"

"It's mine," he tells them in a low voice. He's looking at the floor.

"What's that?"

"He's that senator's boy? You hear me, Joe? The one what makes all the talks raising hell about the federal highway coming through Compton County."

"It's mine! It's mine! It's mine!" He stamps his foot each time he says it.

"Hold on, compadre! Just hold on there. You kindly big to be making such a fuss. How old are you?"

"It's mine," he says now in almost a whisper, his feet still.

"What's yours? What? This? This place?" The Big Man with black hair above his lip, the taller of the two, steps back, moving both his arms from his sides, like he's trying to take flight. "*This palace*? Hee, hee, hee!"

"His daddy must of bought it for him. It must be their vacation home when he ain't in Columbia."

Both of them laugh. The taller one goes to the chair and raises it up. "This yours?" he asks then lets the chair drop back to the floor. "This?" he says, picking up a grime-caked oil lamp. He drops that too. "How about this?" He moves to the old black stove. It's standing alone, quiet. The man goes to it and put his hands on it.

"NO!"

Before he knows it himself, he has hurled himself forward, both his arms in front of him, aimed like an arrow at the Hair-Lipped Big Man. He crashes into the man, his right fist landing in his stomach, his left on his shoulder, and he cannot stop them. They keep moving like piston rods against the man's taut flesh. Then, just as quick, he feels his arms being yanked back and held behind him. The Big Man's eyes are wide and white as eggs and his face is red. He raises his own fist quick and high but it does not move once it's in the air. The fist goes down slowly to his side. "You better be glad you retarded, son, else....But what the hell's so important about a pot-bellied stove that you got to get so fired up about it? Huh?"

"Take a look in it, C.J."

"NO!" He struggles against the blond Big Man but cannot move.

The dark Big Man opens the door of the stove. "My goodness, what have we here?" He reaches in for the sunken mouth of the duffel bag, hanging limply out the door like a tongue, and begins pulling, but the bag sticks on the rim of the mouth and will not move. He pulls harder, squeezing his eyes closed some, until he has managed to wrench the bag loose from the stove. He rocks back some with his effort, stumbling. The bag lands on the floor with a soft *clink*. The man opens it then looks in and smiles. "Well, Joe Davis," he says to the blond Big Man, "I believe old Russell Bankhead here is some kind of Jolly Roger." And then he takes the bag by its mouth and its bottom at the same time and hoists it up, turning it upside down. And the noise begins, the heavy, heavy clattering, the sharp spill, and everything – the knives, the forks, the brass doorknob and bed knob, the key ring without its keys, the sewing needle, the tin plate, the can opener, the tin ashtray and cigarette holder, the brass wedding ring, the nail file – comes down in a quick bright heavy sharp rain, and by the time the rain stops, everything lays on the floor scattered and glittering.

"He ain't nothing but a damned thief!" the blond Big Man says as he holds him tight by the arms.

"I told you! A pirate!"

"A crow's more like it."

"What?"

"A crow. Stealing stuff that shines. Like a crow does."

"*Crow boy!*"

"*Crow boy!*" they cry together.

"It's mine!" he hollers and finally breaks free of the Big Man's grip. He falls on the glowing heap, unmindful of the sharp edges. Then he feels them coming, the tears. He doesn't want them, but they force themselves into his eyes and he buries his face in the pile to hide them. "It's mine!" he says through the tears. He cannot help it. He wants to be a Big Boy, but the tears come.

"What's yours? That pile of shit? Stop crying. Nobody wants *that*."

"Must be a queer, crying over spoons and forks and such as that."

"Yeah he's a queer. Shut up crying. Act your age. Reach down and give him a toke, Joe. Maybe that'll calm him."

"What?"

"I can't stand the sound of crying. Shut up. We don't want your junk. We don't want nothing but to come in here out of the sun and relax. Come on, Joe. Pass that weed over before it goes out."

Their voices back into the corner of the room. He remains on the mound of shining things, protecting it.

"He's kindly pitiful, ain't he?"

"Mmmmmmm."

"How old you reckon he is? Sixteen? Seventeen?"

"I don't know but I think it's funny as hell he is under the impression he owns this house."

The other one says nothing.

"Me and you knows who this house belongs to, don't we, Joe?"

The other one says nothing.

"Maybe we ought to tell him that story. Maybe he ought to know who this house belongs to."

"Shut up, C.J."

"About Nub and you and how this house come to be abandoned...."

"You ain't got to talk about it."

But the other does talk, his voice long and dreamy over the sharp smell of smoke, over the faint glimmers of daylight through the broken windows and rotted shades. And his companion slaps at him with his own voice: "Shut up telling it. Shut up! About Nub Andrews and the money buried under the floorboards and how Joe knowed and come to Nub. Let me have it Nub. Let me have the money or else. Shut up, CJ. He don't need to know. And the fight. The knife flash into Nub's belly. It taking more than a couple of stabs to take him down. He's so big, that Nub, like a hog. Then Nub dead and the money still buried. He'll tell hisself, CJ! Shut the hell up. He'll *tell!*"

He did not know he had slept until the gentle bump of the car's backseat awakens him. The two Big Men are up front, and the day has dimmed to a rusty summer green – the sky ahead of them mud-colored and fading.

"Where?"

He has said it aloud.

"...are we going?"

He thinks of the table at home heaped with Maddie's cooking – the quiet roast and shining sliced tomatoes and sweating glasses of tea and his place there empty with his mother and father sitting quiet and tight-faced, waiting for him, their napkins folded into points in front of them, the blessing not yet said because he is not there.

"We going to get you laid, boy."

"I'd rather lay at home. After I have eaten. Thank you."

Big man laughter from the Dark Big Man. The Blond One sits quiet and tense.

"You ought not have told all that, CJ. He don't need to know."

"He might tell it."

"We'll get him some pussy and he won't think of nothing else. I promise you."

The Blond One looks over the seat at him, his eyes squinting and dark and intense, as though the eyes might come out of his head at him and do him some harm.

The sun is falling down, and the big house sits in the twilight like an old man too lazy to get up and move. They stand in front of the house, the three of them, and the Dark Big Man says to him,

"You got to be on your best behavior in this house, son. This is the meeting place of the high and the mighty, the kings and the princes. No telling who we might run into. So no crying. You hear?"

"We ought not to have brought him, C.J. What if his daddy's in here?"

"Shut up. You'll get him started again."

"Why did you bring him along, C.J.?"

"For fun. Don't you want to have some fun, Joe?"

"Somebody he knows could be here. He could *talk*, C.J."

The Dark Big Man knocks on the door and knocks again and again, and it is only after the third knock that they hear a pair of running feet and see, at the door's small, egg-shaped window, a girl's wide, staring eyes. She looks at them only a second and runs off again, her feet patting swiftly and gently on the floor. "Mavis! Mavis!" they hear her holler. "You won't believe what them two nuts has done gone and done now!"

"Ah hell!" the Dark Big Man says and opens the door himself. They go in and stand in the little dark hall with the bright foot rug and gnarled hat rack. A staircase of polished wood climbs to the next floor to their right, and on their left sits a parlor dressed in mahogany and richly colored carpet.

They hear the staircase creak. A light is on from upstairs, a weak yellow light that barely reaches the bottom steps, and a woman comes down in a bathrobe. She takes her time descending, and when she reaches the middle of the staircase, she stops and faces the three of them. She does not look like a nice lady. She has white hair like Gravel Gertie's, and her face is wrinkled and lined and hard. She is thin. She folds her arms across herself and waits.

"Hey lady!" the Dark Big Man says.

"Who the hell is that?" the woman asks in a low voice.

"It's a special guest of ours, Mavis."

"It's a youngun, and he can't stay here."

"How come he can't?"

"How come? Because he's goddamned underage. That's how come. Have you lost your mind, Charlie?"

"I told you, C.J. We ought not to brought him."

"Ought not use the Lord's name in vain in front of a youngun, Mavis. Might influence him the wrong way."

"Shut up and get him out of here. You get out too, for that matter! You and your smart mouth. I don't need it tonight."

"No ma'am. We ain't going no place. I ain't had my pipes cleaned in three weeks, Mavis. I'm all backed up and ready to bust."

"Get out now!"

"What you going to do if we don't? Call the police? I'd like to see that. We got money. Look here, Mavis." The Dark Big Man reaches into his pocket and pulls out his wallet and opens it. "Got paid today. Got money to spend. Ah. I knew the sight of money would soften you up, Mavis. Money always smoothes folks over."

"Well, that youngun's not going anywhere near them girls. You hear me?"

"And how come? We brung him here to give him some experience and make a man of him. This is his *initiation*."

"He stays here in the parlor, or you don't see nobody tonight. Understand? Now which girls do you want to see?"

"I believe Sally the Sword Swallower will cure what ails me. She in tonight, Mavis? Good. How about you, Joe?"

The Blond One stands silent till the Dark Big Man prods him on the shoulder. "I don't know. I'm kindly out of the mood now."

"Out of the mood?"

"Mavis is right. We ought not brought that youngun."

"Oh God Almighty! Well, you stay down here and watch him then, all right? If you so worried about him. I'm going upstairs."

There is a moment of silence. Then the Blond One says, "No, no. I'll go upstairs. Dorothea here tonight, Mavis?"

The woman turns without a word and goes up the stairs.

They leave him alone at the foot of the stairs. He turns to the parlor and enters it and walks about its shadowy coolness. A pair of heavy-shaded lamps light the room in each corner. Between them sits a couch, nearly big as an automobile, with great fat red cushions leaning against each plush arm. A low, dark mahogany coffee table precedes the couch. Another piece of mahogany, parallel to the couch and coffee table, holds a square box atop it. He goes to the box and sees that it is a record player with a disc already on it and the needle perched dead on the rim of the vinyl record. He leans down to read the title, but it is too dark in the room and all he can make out is one word, MAN. He turns from the player, and as soon as he turns, just at the moment of his swivel, he catches the sight, the flash, the glitter. His eye catches it but so do his insides: the sun is almost down now, but a long red finger of it points through the dense-curtained windows of the parlor, as though directing him to something, and he follows the thin finger, and there, on the mantelpiece, above the black, deep-throated fireplace, it sits, a small, glittering mirror, throwing off sparks as what's left of the sun hits it. He goes to the mirror right away, nearly runs to it, and takes it down from the mantel. It's not heavy at all, not as much as you might think upon first seeing it. The glass itself is set in brass that runs around it and holds it in loops; lion's feet protrude at the bottom, brassy and bright as well. He sees his face in the glass, but he doesn't want to see it. He presses the mirror to his chest. "Oh, it'll shine so good," he says to himself. "When the sun hits it, all of the sun, the mirror and the brass, oh it will shine like a little sun itself! Lord, don't let the sun go out yet. I want to see the glass burn. The brass. The lion's feet." He holds it over his head, aimed at the window, so that the last of the red sun can touch it and set it aflame.

"You best put that back," a voice says in the dark. He turns to see that it is a woman, but not the same woman as before. She turns on the big light, and the sun is gone now, for good. It is a younger woman, and she is holding something in her right hand which she now offers to him. "Let's make a trade. You take this and I'll take that." She takes the mirror from him with her free hand and gives him the black, cold bottle of Coke. "It's got ice on it and everything." She has the mirror in both hands and she lifts it to put it back on the mantel. "You drop that, and Miss Rains will skin us both alive. Now drink your drink. Go on. Sit down and drink it." She has hair like the Big Blond Man, a gold-white kind of color that could well shine in the sun. Her face is thin and sad and there are big purple shadows under her dark eyes.

"What's your name? You can tell me. Don't be shy. I'll tell you mine. My real name is Mary Elizabeth, but around here they call me Venus Fly Trap. Yes. Isn't that nasty? The boys give all us girls names, whether we like it or not. And what can we do to stop them? They're trash, most of them. Some good ones. Some gentlemen. But not many. Certainly not the two you come in with. What are you doing with trash like that? They been in jail and everything, more than one time, since they were boys. Are they your friends? They said you was a senator's boy or something. Are you? Don't be shy. You know Joe, the blond headed one? He's an idiot. Thinks he killed somebody. C.J. got him real drunk one night and convinced him he killed old Nub Andrews on the other side of Beaslap. Stabbed him to death. When old Nub got burned alive in a house fire some five miles down the road in a whole different house altogether. But Joe believes it to this day he killed Nub and that nobody but him and C.J. knows. That's how dumb Joe is and how mean C.J. is. C.J. kind of hypnotized him. It's a way for him to keep a hold on Joe, I reckon. Why is it you keep looking over my shoulder? Good Lord, what's so special about this mirror that it fascinates you so?" She takes it from the mantel and holds it in front of her. "I think it's kind of ugly myself. All them gnarls. But Mavis says a very special friend of hers gave it to her as a gift, so she keeps it and in a prominent place too."

She does not set it back over the fireplace but leans down and puts in on the long dark table in front of him. "Here, you can look at it all you like. You just can't have it."

She hushes for a moment, but he is not watching her, for in front of him, on the table, it sits, the mirror, quiet too and not shining now at all. It's turned up a little bit on its hinges, so he can see part of the ceiling in it. He wants to reach out so bad and snatch it. It's so close! He would take it out when the sun was high and bright and sit it on some bald spot on the ground, away from grass and dirt and rocks, and let the sun fall on it. It would shine, boy! Oh yes! The mirror and the brass would go up like a flame, like durned gold fire! And he would not hide it away in a pot-bellied stove but keep it out for everyone to see. He would take it with him everywhere, even to school. It shines better than anything else, he would tell Miss Gatlin. Better than the sun!

"You got a nice face, the woman starts up again," but he still doesn't watch her. "You have a girlfriend? I'll bet you're old enough to have one. Well, you won't have no trouble getting one, that's for sure, you being a politician's son and all. You won't have a problem getting anything you want. You got it made. I used to have it made. You believe me? Well, it's true. I was married once to this peach farmer, the richest man in Compton County. Years ago. But I didn't love him, and he didn't love me, just my being young and pretty. He would have given me anything I wanted, clothes and jewelry and trips everywhere. It's true. But I was miserable and I ran away. I was just a youngun and I wanted to act like a youngun and be around other young people, young men. So I left the money, the clothes, everything. Wrote them a note and told them I was going to Atlanta, but I didn't. I didn't get any farther than Greenville. Went to work at an old dive there, not much better than this place. Got married to the manager, who was old too, like my first husband, and I left him as well. And I came right back here. But that's not my point. My point is that I could have had it made too, like you, if I could have sit still and looked pretty and not wanted to be young, only *look* young for this old man. You're not going to drink that, are you, and it's making a ring on the table. Lord, Miss Rains will have a fit! Here, let me have it and I'll put it back up." She takes the Coke and leaves the room, leaves him alone with the mirror, quiet and unshining in its frame. He leans forward, so that he is almost over it, close enough so that his breath could stain it if he breathes hard enough.

"Anyway," the woman says upon her return to the parlor, "my mama had no right pushing me into that first marriage. It was all her doing, her wanting to be surrounded by finery. I was just a child, you know. Hey, best leave that mirror alone, I told you. You break it, and Miss Rains will have both our scalps. Here. I better put it back. She takes it and sets it back over the fireplace. Strange a boy your age would be interested in such as that." She crosses her arms over herself and looks toward the window, which is dark with new night. "I never had a young boyfriend. Not in all these years. Never knew what it was like to be loved by a boy. I know older men have the wisdom and know how and all, but young men are so *alive*, so fresh and bright – their skin and their hair, their voices even. So pretty. My first husband was fifty-seven years old, and the one after him was forty-five. What draws them to me, or me to them? Anyway, I'm too old for young romance now. You know how old I am? Take a guess. Won't you guess? Well, I'll tell you then. I am *forty-seven* years old. That's right. People say I don't look it, but that's how old I am. Too old for a youngun. Besides, the young want the young. The boys never ask for me when they come in. Only the old." She steps away from the fireplace, leaving the mirror bare on the mantel. "Look at me," she says, closer to him now. "Look! I wouldn't have told nobody but you my age. You know that? Because you're so *quiet*. Not even Miss Rains knows it, although I imagine she suspects. You're sweet. Sweet and quiet. I can't believe you don't have a girlfriend. A young lady ought to snatch you right up. You're so pretty. Your mouth. Your cheeks. Your cheeks have roses in them. Oh, ha. Have you ever been kissed? Look at me! That's right. I'm not so bad to look at, even at forty-seven years old. I'll kiss you. I'll be your first." She comes closer to him, leaning down. He feels her breath and hair close to his cheek, her mouth covering his.

Now, he lies on the ground looking up at the bashful stars, which wink only now and then. The automobile is several feet away. Its radio is turned up loud, and the sound of twanging voices and twanging music echoes in the wooded grove by the water where they are parked. IT WASN'T GOD WHO MADE HONKY TONK ANGELS! The Dark Big Man, the taller of the two, sits there smoking on the left runner of the car, the driver's door wide open. His smoke drifts up to the blue-black night sky and makes the stars fuzzy in places. At some point the music stops and is replaced by a Big Man's voice, deep and serious, telling how the President of the United States has suffered a heart attack in Denver, Colorado.

"Goddamn!" the Dark Big Man shouts. "They'll interrupt the goddamn music for any goddamn thing." As though hearing him, the music comes back, as loud and twangy as before. – THE WILD, WILD SIDE OF LIFE!

He doesn't care if the music stops or not. He doesn't care about anything else, because, under his shirt he has it hidden, the mirror, and now he brings it out and lays it beside him on the grass. He took it in their last few moments in the house, when the girls came down the stairwell, naked, their skin white as eggshells, chasing both Big Men in front of them, cursing them, hitting at them with their hands. "Money, money, our money," they had screamed, and the Dark Big Man had looked around and hit back at them with the back of his hand and said it wasn't worth a dime much less forty dollars, and then came the woman, the owner of the house, and there was even more noise and commotion and tussling from side to side. Names called. Things thrown down and broken. Mary, the woman who had kissed him, joined in, and that's when he went to the mantel and snatched the mirror from it and took off for outdoors and the backseat of the Big Men's car. They followed soon after, putting on their shirts as they walked and looking back at the women in the lighted doorway, cursing at them the whole time.

He had the mirror!

It was on the grass now beside him, full of the sky and the stars and the tops of the black trees. Tomorrow though, when the sun was out, it would shine! Oh boy. Like fire! He would stand and hold it high up and let the gold light pour.

"You will tell."

He didn't hear the voice at first. He was staring into the black depths of the mirror, with its pin points of white light, star light.

"C.J. ought not have brung you along."

He turns. It is the Blond Big Man standing over him, looking down, his hair lit by the dark but his eyes even blacker and blanker than the eye of the mirror.

"Ought not to have had nothing to do with you. Ought to have left you alone."

"You will tell. I know it."

"You can't help what you do. You don't know no better."

A click somewhere, a clean, swift sound. Then up from the man's side comes the blade, visible only by its point.

"You'll tell and it will all come out and that will be it for me. They'll fry my ass. God damn. And I didn't get to enjoy none of it. Didn't even get the money." His voice breaks.

He steps closer. He stoops some, right above him, his knees bent. His arm rises. The blade catches light from some source in the night sky, enough to make it flash as it comes down.

"Oh it shines so good, boy!"

What A Jezebel Looks Like

If I never say nothing else in my life that's true, they's one thing I can say for sure and be satisfied about it: Men is dogs and always have been dogs and always will be dogs. And that's that! Look at your Bible. Look at your history. Look at the way men has done women from all the way back yonder to all the way up here, in the year nineteen-forty-seven! I don't have time to list 'em all. Let me just say that the worst hounds in the pack undoubtedly belong right here in Compton, South Carolina, right here in the McMillan clan!

You McMillan boys has got into all your trouble for one reason and one reason alone: the fact you cannot and will not keep your trousers shut!

All of you. You. Earl. George. Russell. Harry. Clayton. The only McMillan that ain't got a problem keeping good sense around a woman is Bert-Etta, and that's 'cause she IS a woman! Earl married and divorced twicet and him not even forty years old yet. George and that Singleton woman all mixed up and shameful and her barely out of the bassinet good. Clayton too drunk to know if he's sleeping with Sarah or some tramp from Broadusville. Lord knows what Russell and Harry's got into, but nothing would surprise me. And you too, Bert McMillan. Yes you. I know. All about you and Theresa. Don't try to lie. Fact of business, I have done been in touch with Theresa about it this very afternoon. Said my piece to her about you and her and this thing y'all got going on. Or had going on, I should say, for it's a finished thing now. I reckon you won't be quite as attracted to her after today. You might want to go down the road and take a look at her. See for yourself what I'm talking about.

I had heard talk now and then over the years about you and your little girlfriends. Whispers and such as that. They some people can't live and breathe lessen they causing trouble for other folks. Even had a friend come to me oncet in the mill and ask me if I knowed about you and so-and-so. Told her to go jump in the lake and not ever come round me talking like that again. It bothered me some at first, this talk, sure. What woman wouldn't have been bothered to hear her husband ain't been quite as faithful as he claimed, lessen she was made out of rock or something? On the other hand, I thought, "Goody-good if he's getting it on the side. That's less work and bother for me." But then Theresa's name got into it. Theresa Whitley! My sister-in-law. More a sister than a sister-in-law. My best friend in the world. That's how close we been. Practically blood kin. You know that. We growed up together in Gaffney. Come to Compton about the same time. Lived two houses down from each other for all these years. Talked everyday if we didn't visit in person. Natural enough, I didn't want to believe such a thing no matter how much I might have heard. Not about Theresa.

But then I found out for myself. From you, Bert McMillan. That's right. I woke up that night. Heard voices. One voice. Yours. Thought you might have been talking to Emory or Bertie Mae or Ruth. Maybe one of them was sick or scared and you were comforting them so's they'd go back to bed and get back to sleep. I got up and went to the den but stopped at the bedroom door to listen. You was in the dark with the phone to your ear and talking. And I heard what you said. Not all of it. But enough. And I heard her name. You let her name drop in the dark, and I heard and knowed what was going on. Went back to bed but didn't sleep. When you got back in beside me a few minutes later thinking I was sleeping, I prayed I didn't sniffle too loud to let you know I wasn't.

What A Jezebel Looks Like

The next morning I went about everything – getting dressed, making your breakfast, everything – wondering if in the long run it really mattered that you and Theresa was seeing each other behind mine and Ed's back. Did I really, really care? More important, had I loved you in the first place? Enough to marry you, I reckon. But I wasn't even sure about that. You was good-looking enough when I met you. Had that hard McMillan jawline. And was put together well-enough. Looked good and solid in a military man's uniform. Sort of like Gary Cooper but a few notches down. But it takes more than good looks for a good woman to love a man, really love him. To find him good enough for her love so she loves him for keeps. You worked hard. Always had. And went to church, till right recently. Least-ways you'd been baptized and didn't cuss all that much. Now and then. But not enough to give offense to a Christian girl or her daddy. But you was peculiar. Still are peculiar. Going off by yourself so much, even here in the house, when I'm here nearby and might like to talk to you. You go to the kitchen and set at the table like it's suppertime, when it's not, not for hours. Or on the porch. Never ask me to come and set out there with you. What are you doing by yourself, Bert? Thinking? And thinking of what? Other women? Theresa Whitley?

Well, it's a new day, Bert McMillan, and I done put away my wondering and my worrying. Done shut out the whispering of others and what they might mean. I roused myself this morning, fixed your breakfast, seen you off to the mill, then left this house in the very blaze of the hot summer sun and walked right down to Ed and Theresa's. Didn't say a word to nobody. Didn't have words in me good enough to say how I felt, just powerful-feeling anger and righteousness. Went up Ed and Theresa's front porch. Didn't knock at the door. We don't knock, you know. We kinfolk. We just go on in. So I went on in. Theresa was at the kitchen sink doing her dishes.

"Hey!" I says.

She turns and sees me and wipes her hands on her apron. She knows something's up. "You all right?" she says.

"No," I says back and without saying nothing else grab holt of her pretty brown hair and yank it so hard she hollers. But I don't let go. No sir. I ain't done with her yet. She's a-yelping like a bitch in heat, and I just keep holt of her by the scalp and move the both of us toward the front door. It's like we're locked together, hand to head, with no chance of getting loose from one another. Pretty soon I turn and haul her behind me like I would a bag of garbage I was carrying out to the curb. We going outdoors. I want the whole of Byrd Street, as many people as who might be outside right then, to see what a Jezebel looks like. A genuine Bathsheba. The whore of Babylon! Don't need to go to the movie show to see her. Don't need no Barbara Stanwyck or Bette Davis. Here's a real-life one right here in Compton, South Carolina! All you got to do is turn and look-see. Get you a eye full.

I get her and me out to the front yard and set down in the grass, right plumb near the edge of the road, hoping to God as many cars as there is in Compton would drive by and see us. Miss Jennilee Gentry's on her front porch in her rocking chair, spitting snuff through her first two fingers now and then and watching it land in the dirt. She probably thinks me and Theresa has done gone crazy, acting like a couple of younguns in the grass. Which is fine. We are crazy. At least I am, crazy with hate for a woman I thought I could trust.

I'm on the ground, and I pull down Theresa across my lap. She's short but a little stocky, so it hurts some. But I don't care. It's a good hurt. A righteous hurt. I pull up her dress so her bloomers shows, and I set about whupping the tar out of your little girlfriend, like she's a youngun that's done something awful wrong. She's worse than that in my book. Miss Gentry's done stood up by now to make sure she's seeing what she's seeing and it ain't the sweet-tasting Checkerberry put fool notions in front of her eyes. She don't know whether to laugh or call the law or what. "It's all right, Jennilee," I says to her. "She's earned it. And if you stick around till about five o'clock, you'll see Bert McMillan get hissen too."

I ain't going to hit you, Bert. Not now leastways. The notion might take me later. But not now. That's just something I said to Jennilee to make for a better show. You might have a weak conscience, but you still got strong hands, and if you hit me with them, I'd have to kill you, I reckon. For a man that lays a hand on me won't be a live man for very long afterward. Nah. I ain't going to touch you. And you ain't touching me either. Ever again. Long as we live together. Your woman-touching days is over and done with.

In Spring The Sun Will Smell Like Roses

Mama always says that in spring the sun will smell like roses. I have never been sure what she means by that, but this time, when it began to look and feel like spring, when something in my bones just told me spring had come (there are no calendars in the house, Mama won't allow them) and the sun was bright in the blue sky, I was anxious to go outdoors and find out for myself if what she said is true. Mama never would let me before. She's always been the one to go outside for things, not me nor my sister (when my sister was still living here). "Don't doubt me," Mama always says. And that is that. So I have had to imagine the sun putting out a scent as sweet as what comes off them red and white petals.

"Don't doubt me," Mama always said, but I did then and I still do. I am outdoors now for the first time in a long time, sweeping the porch on a clear day in May. (Mama's asleep in the den while a TV show plays in front of her, so I take my chance.) The sun stands right above me, bright as a peach, but I don't smell anything but what the broom has stirred up. If it is true what Mama says about the sun and all, wouldn't I smell it? The sun's a big old thing up yonder in the sky. Surely to goodness that rose smell would come down to me from something so huge. Surely it would radiate throughout our yard and the whole neighborhood for that matter. But there's nothing, only dust and dirt and the faint smell of 'zaleas from the windowsill planters.

I slip back inside the house and say, "Mama, I just don't smell it. Don't mean to doubt you or nothing, but I don't smell roses out yonder." Mama's not listening though, just laying on the couch looking up at nothing in particular, not even listening to the TV that plays right next to her. It's not like her to be so idle. Usually she is up and about, going here and yonder, in and out, never stopping. "Can't stop," she said once when someone asked her about it. "Got to keep going for my babies." By my babies she meant me and Rosemarie, when Rosemarie was still here. Rosemarie's gone now. Two men in bright white suits fetched her in her wheelchair and carried her off, with Rosemarie just a-crying and Mama behind the three of them hollering, "You can't take her! She don't belong to you!" (I tell you what: them two men come into the house like a bolt of lightning from out of nowhere and was gone just as fast. Scared me the way lightning always does when I see it outside my window.) I never figured out full-ways why they come for Rosemarie. Just got hints of why. Neglect was a word I heard. I just figured they took her because it got too hard for me and Mama to look after her. Mama ain't young no more. Neither am I, although Mama says I am. "You'll always be my little girl no matter how old you get," she says, and to show she means it, at Christmastime she gives me a new baby doll. That's right. A right handsome looking thing too. Almost tall as a real person with a bow in its yellow hair and a pretty skirt and shoes. I got a whole room full of dolls by now. Lined up against my bedroom wall like a little troop of girlie soldiers. I turn on the light and they just startle me, sitting there all in a row, just a –staring, like they expect something from me – a whole long line of shiny eyes and shiny smiles and pretty dresses. There are even some Barbie dolls mixed in with the other ones, but they've been swallowed up in the silk swirls of the bigger dolls and peek around the hemlines here and there like they are afraid to be noticed. Mama says, "You stay with your old mama, and you'll get a new doll every Christmas." I guess that's one good thing about Rosemarie being gone: I get all Mama's attention and all the presents at Christmas.

"But dolls is for girls," I said once to her.

"You are a girl," she said back.

That's when I raised my hands to show the black spots on the tops of them. "Girls ain't got hands like these. These is an old woman's hands. And my face is an old woman's face. And my hair. Everything, Mama!"

Mama just shook her head real quick-like and said, "It don't matter about your hands or your face or your hair. You'll always be your mama's little girl. You'll always have a home here with your mama."

"I'm old, Mama, and so are you!"

Mama just shook her head like something had got loose in her hair and she was trying to be rid of it. And then she walked off from me.

I must say that Rosemarie did become quite a burden there by the end. She was old too and had gotten heavy, and she couldn't do nothing for herself. Had the palsy. Was all twisted up from head to foot. Couldn't even finish a sentence she had started. We had to do that for her too. She'd try to strain out a few words but then gave up, and me and Mama had to complete her thought for her. Worst part was getting her to the bathroom when she had to do a bad job. Me and Mama got all red-faced and trembly-like lifting her out of her chair and on to the pot so's she could go both ways, front and back, at the same time. Then we'd have to lift her up, clean her up good, and get her back into her chair. Then Mama'd cover the pot and take it outdoors to get rid of it, bury it. We never did leave a bad job in the house. None of us. Mama doesn't trust plumbing and is scared of germs. Mighty scared. She is always washing her hands. Got us to doing it too. Got so's our hands are red as a rooster comb sometimes. Mama washes after almost everything she does. Where she takes the bad jobs, I don't know. Off into the woods for burial, I reckon. I have offered to help her time and again tote them, but she always says no, says it's best for me to stay in the house.

If Daddy was still around all this wouldn't be such a chore, I reckon. Mama says he's no good. Never has been. Never will be. I don't know. I knew him when he was a young man, right before he left us. He was young and filled-out looking – with muscles, I reckon – and I can't imagine but that he did nothing but get stronger as he got older. He was strong enough to hit Mama one time. I remember that. His hand went quick as lightning across her face. I can still remember the snap. It was like a flash that came and went so fast it was almost like it didn't happen in the first place. Fact of business, it took Mama a few seconds to figure out she'd just been hit. Then she put her hand to the offended cheek and started to cry. She cried a lot back then. That's because her and Daddy got into it so much. Fussing. About everything, it seems like. But mostly about Daddy. How he drank too much and laid out of work too much and spent too much time with his men friends and all that. They'd fight something awful sometimes. Their voices climbed over each other to see which could reach the highest. Daddy could holler high as a woman if he got mad enough. It scared me and Rosemarie when they got to arguing. We'd go off in a corner someplace and just huddle and tremble in each other's arms. Sometimes we expected the roof of the house to come down on us. That's how bad it could get. And it would usually end with Daddy saying, "Well maybe it's time you found you somebody else, 'cause that's what I aim to do." And he'd go tromping out the front door like he was leaving for good. But around midnight or so, he'd be back. Drunk as a skunk. Mama would hug him and things would be all right again for a while.

But one time he didn't come back. Didn't call or write or anything. Mama paced the house front and back, every room, outdoors too, like she expected him to come shambling up the steps, tearfully telling her he was sorry and asking to come back *one more time Elsie please!* But he never did.

"I-i-i-s h-e-e-e dead?" Rosemarie asked in that lopsided, stuttering way of hers, finally spitting out the words.

"Might as well be," Mama answered. "I hope he is! Oh I don't know! I don't know!" and she broke into tears. "See what happens when you leave home?" she said through her crying. "When you go out into the world and give your trust to somebody else? Nothing good comes from it. Nothing!"

That got Rosemarie to crying. She put her pale hands to her face and cried out, "D-d-d-on't s-s-s-s-ay th-th-th-at! D-d-d-on't!" Like there was any chance for her to get far in the world in her condition.

(Sometimes I wonder, even with her condition and all, if it wasn't Rosemarie who somehow got in touch with those men in white and told them to come get her. Maybe she's the one who accused Mama of neglect. I can't say for sure. She sure didn't do it in front of me or ever ask me to help her. But the thought has crossed my mind right often. Goodness knows it would have been one way to get out of this house.)

When me and Rosemarie were younger, and when Daddy was around more and before he left for good, of course, we used to get out a fair bit. Go all around town and the county. Go to the fair in the fall and the July 4th picnic in the summertime in city park. Go to the mountains to watch how gold and red the leaves had got. Even went to the beach at least twice in my recollection. I can still remember Mama young and pretty back then in her one-piece bathing suit. Her dark hair was cut short, and she just laughed at everything Daddy said. I can picture her: the ocean rolling behind her in big, fat waves and Mama's mouth wide open, her white teeth shining at some joke Daddy made. They didn't holler at each other so much then. That came later. When Daddy drank too much and couldn't keep a job. When Mama's nerves got bad and every little thing riled her up, even the ringing of the telephone. That's when we stopped going places, when me and Rosemarie seemed to lose the world for good to the four walls of this little house.

We didn't go anywhere or see anybody. And nobody came to see us. If they did, if some salesman showed or something, she'd send me and Rosemarie to our room till "the danger" was passed. Why? Was there something the matter with us? That's what I asked her once. She got red-faced and said, "No, it's not you. It's them. The other person. People are nasty things. They carry germs everywhere they go. You want that? Huh? No, I didn't rightly think so."

Once though, I did run into some other folks. Well, they showed at the door. This was after they took Rosemarie away. Mama was in town at the grocery store. Someone knocked at the door. "Don't ever answer if I'm not here!" Mama always said. There were three shadows against the front door curtain, and whoever it was just peeped around and peeped around, and they saw me. I was going to run for my room, but through an opening in the curtain they saw me and wiggled me over with a little finger. I went. I shouldn't have, but I couldn't help it. It was something new for me, and I just had to do it. So I opened the door, and there stood three black people in the door way, a man and two women. The man looked old with gray hair fuzzing his head and his chin, but he had a nice, big bright smile. The women looked a lot younger. They were all dressed to the nines, the man in a coat and tie, the women in long dresses that reached past their knees.

"Ah, young lady," the man began, and there was a whistling through his teeth. "May we come in a moment and share with you the saving knowledge of our Lord and Savior, Jesus Christ?"

"Who are you?" I asked.

"We are Jehovah's Witnesses, representatives of the truth that will save mankind from its own insidious destruction."

I noticed they carried things in their hands, the women anyway. Programs or brochures with The Watchtower printed on them and Awake!

"I ain't supposed to let strangers in the house. Ain't even supposed to talk to them."

"Ah, little sister, when all is said and done, you and I are not strangers but sister and brethren in the family of our Lord."

Well, that sounded good enough, I reckoned, and they were mighty interesting looking people, so I stepped aside and let them in, and the man thanked me very much and the pretty women followed him, and we sat around the den while the man spoke of the coming destruction of the world, on the ruins of which God would build His holy and lasting kingdom. It just fascinated me the way he talked, like somebody from way up and faraway.

It wasn't too long, though, when Mama reappeared, her arms loaded down with grocery bags. She didn't show any Christian charity to our visitors. She wasn't about to accept this man or those women as family. She dropped the groceries to the floor. Apples rolled out of bags and something broke inside a sack. Her face was blood-red and she shook. "Who are you?" she asked, but didn't give the gentleman time to explain. Not at all. He tried to tell her who they were and why they were there, but she wasn't going to hear it. She ran the three of them out with threats of calling the police. She even shoved at them some till they were all gone and the door was closed behind them. Then she faced me, her cheeks no less red.

"Don't you ever. And I mean EVER let anyone through that door again without me being here. Do you understand? Do you know what they could have done to you if I hadn't come in? They could have cut your throat and took everything we have. Are you crazy, child? What have I told you all these years about *strangers*? I don't care if it's coloreds or whites. You can't trust people!"

I did go to school for a while till I was old enough to quit. Then Mama quit for me, saying I had to help the family out by going to work. But I didn't. I stayed home with her, always wondering when my new job, my *first* job, would start. It never did. Rosemarie went to a special school in another town and made it all the way through. Got a diploma and everything. Then she came home and stayed. There was no school good enough to prepare *her* for a job. What in the world would she have been able to do? Nothing. Not a thing.

When I did quit school I kept some of the books, maybe five. Kept them under my bed or some other secret place. Mama didn't like me having books. Said reading was bad for the eyes, would weaken them, and I'd go blind while I was still young. We don't even have a Bible around here that I know of.

"Like Helen Keller?" I asked her once, but she only looked at me funny and walked away.

My favorite book was called A Young Person's Atlas of the United States. It was a long book and very wide and the hardest one to hide. I liked the map of South Carolina the most, probably since that's where I live. It amazed me to realize what a big place South Carolina was, bigger than some big cities and famous cities, I reckon. I had imagined up to then that there was just this place where we lived, this little town, and that was South Carolina and there was nothing else to it. But the map told different. I put my finger on the spot on the map where we were and traced it by the small lines and the bigger ones, the red ones and green ones and whites, like all kind of veins in a body part, to all the other cities in the state. Greenville and Columbia and Charleston and Myrtle Beach. It about took my breath away to realize there was so much else to what I used to think was so small.

When I asked Mama about Charleston and Myrtle Beach and the others, she looked at me twisted-ways and said, "How come you asking about *that*?" I shrugged. Didn't have an answer to that, not one she would like anyway. She didn't answer either, so after a while I just left her, more curious than I had been before.

She caught me with the book eventually. One night. I had it out on the floor with a lamp beside me just a-studying that crooked little state where I live. It looked like a wedge of pie that hadn't been cut straight. And I loved it and wanted to see more of it, to see where those long lines led and was determined to do so. That's when Mama came in. She stopped in the door a moment, adjusted her eyes to the dark that ate up the room, then came swooping down on me.

"I told you!"

The two of us fought over that book. Yes sir. Played tug of war with it. I was a big girl by then, a real big girl, maybe sixteen or seventeen. Maybe older. At some point I lost count. We don't celebrate birthdays anymore. Except Jesus Christ's. Anyway, I was a good match for Mama and about had the book out of her hands. But she beat me and clutched it tightly to her.

"I done told you reading would ruin your eyes!"

I was mad, madder than I'd ever been in my entire life.

"Damn you!" I said, the first time I ever cussed. The last too. I let loose all kind of hateful words at Mama right then. Told her I wished she would die, that I would die, that I could be where they took Rosemarie, that this house would burn down right now. You'd think Mama, being as strong as she is, could have taken that kind of sass or that she would have marched right over and beaten the devil right out of me. But no. She stood quiet a moment before this look came upon her face. It was like she'd seen the boogeyman or something. And maybe she had. Anyway the look of fear crumpled into one of sadness, and she went to crying right then with that atlas still cradled in her arms. I realized in a flash how much I had hurt her, like my daddy used to do. And I felt like the single worst human being on the face of the earth.

Mama left the room but soon came back.

"You know," she said, her eyes still shining with tears (she wasn't holding the atlas anymore), "you only got one mama, and what in the world would you do if I wasn't here? Huh? How would you get along? You got nobody else but me, and when I'm gone…" She didn't finish what she was saying. She just turned and strolled slowly out of the room and left me alone with a single light burning near my bed.

There was another time before that when Mama liked to have caught me with my books. She is deathly afraid of thunderstorms. Always has been, she says, since she was a little girl and was raised out in the open where the lightning was so big and clear and the thunder loud as cannon fire. Even when Daddy was here and it came up a cloud, she would panic and try to get us all into the middle of the house or to lay together on her and Daddy's bed. Daddy wouldn't go along with it though. Sometimes he spited her by going out on the front porch while the thunder and lightning cracked all around us. After he was gone and it came up a cloud, we'd go into the hall or into her bedroom and lay together. Even Rosemarie. We had to lift her out of her chair and get her on the bed with us. One time, though, Mama led us into Rosemarie's and my room, because it was the furtherest room in the house. It was a real bad cloud, and Mama was scared a tornado might drop out of it. So we didn't get on my and Rosemarie's bed. We got under it. And it was under it that I had stashed away the books I took from school, including that atlas of the United States. It was me first, and I scrunched real close to the wall where the books were. Then it was Rosemarie beside me and Mama last. Lord, I was scared to death Mama might see those books or smell them or whatever. I was more scared of that than any thunderstorm cutting up outside. I held my breath for what seemed like maybe thirty minutes, although I know it couldn't have been that long, and I felt the greatest relief of my life when that storm rolled over and we got up from under that bed.

But Mama is right, you know. All I have is her. If something happened to her –

I never learned to do anything. She wouldn't let me. Never learned to cook or sew or drive an automobile. She said I didn't have to, what with her being there to do everything for me, happy to do it, she always said. I had one purpose in life and have one purpose now: to stay in this house and make sure my mama doesn't feel the awful loneliness that was left to her by my daddy and by my sister. Some folks might say I'm lucky that way. Some folks might even call me a queen, getting waited on hand and foot by a woman who says she loves me more than life itself.

The night Mama took the book from me, I went to bed mighty, mighty afraid of things. Everything. Of what could be. I reckon if she wanted, Mama could walk off the way Daddy did or go away the same as Rosemarie. I went to trembling that night and cried and promised the Lord I never would sass-talk my mama again, that I would respect her and appreciate her and accept her every show of kindness with gratitude. That next morning as she was drinking her coffee at the kitchen table, I went down on my knees and told her of the promise I made to God. And I kissed her knees and her hands and her face and said over and over again, "Thank you, Mama! Thank you, thank you for all you have done!" You have never seen a happier person in your whole life. Mama, I mean. She set down her coffee cup and pulled me to her, and the both of us had a good, long, strong cry.

And I kept the promise. For how long? I couldn't tell you, except long enough to put black spots on the backs of my hands and silver in my hair.

A very long time, I reckon.

And Mama has just worked and worked all these long years – worked like a horse. She's tuckered out now. Has been on that couch for a good while. That's how come I went out to sweep the porch – to help her out a little bit. And to smell the sun too. I don't imagine Mama minds it any. She hasn't gotten on to me so far about being outdoors. She just lays on that couch and stares at whatever is in front of her. She's still so pretty. Wrinkled some now and gray. But she's still the prettiest lady I ever laid eyes on. Doesn't even say anything either. She's earned this peace and quiet with what all she's been through.

Except it doesn't feel like peace and quiet. Nor smell like it either. It smells like something else, something bad, and I drop the broom and run my hands up to my mouth.

"Mama!" I call out. There's a catch in my throat. I'm crying. My heart and my brain know something they won't tell me yet. Or maybe I just refuse to hear it.

"Mama. Haven't I been a good girl to you? A good daughter? I stayed with you when Daddy and Rosemarie left."

She doesn't hear me. She's gone off someplace without me. Maybe if I look where she looks and follow it, I can find where she's gone.

"Mama, I don't know what I'll do here by myself."

So I sit down beside her and watch her eyes and do my best to find out where she's got to.

A Plinth of Night

Every night he watched them, this strange trio, the two men and the woman (that is what it looked like, a woman, that is what it appeared to be in the darkness), make their way by foot along the side of the highway and go over the railroad tracks and disappear to goodness knew where. Then, maybe an hour or two later, they would return the exact way they had come, except the men would be toting cloth sacks loaded with something, and he could almost hear them, even across the road, grunt and groan with their new burden.

The woman did not make the trip by foot, however, because she had no feet, and she did not carry a sack because she did not have arms to balance such a weight. She was mainly a torso, a miniature trunk with a large head of whitish, that the men had secured to this kind of trundling table, this flat, round surface that moved upon rollers. It reminded him of an altar, a plinth, and the woman, if that's what she was, was a kind of malformed deity being pushed back and forth by its subalterns. He could pick out her deformities in the successive electric lights secured by cedar poles along the road and because he had excellent eyesight, twenty-twenty vision. She had legless feet and armless hands, all of which appeared useless and incapable of motion. She wore the same colored dress night after night with the sleeves and legs cut away to allow her stumps to "breathe." The two men with her appeared young and scruffy. Each sported full beards and wore caps and denim shirts and blue jeans. They were slender and long-limbed.

He didn't know these people. He didn't know many people in that town. He was newly arrived there and had taken a job as a night watchman at the local hardware store. The store had suffered a number of break-ins of late, despite the installation of surveillance equipment, and the owners hired someone to keep a watch on it. He didn't know if the job would be permanent or not, and it didn't offer very much money. More than likely he would have to find another job during the day regardless of what happened with this one. But it was a start. That was how he looked at it: a new beginning. He had had some trouble in his former hometown in the county next to this one, involving drinking and drugs and not being able to hold a steady job. His mother and father, truly broken up about the situation, had reminded him that he was no child anymore. In fact, he was close to thirty years old. It was time he grew up and took care of himself. And afterwards, with tears in their eyes and hoarse voices, they showed him the door out of their house. It was all right. He understood and didn't hate them for it. They were right. So he moved south, thirty miles down the road, to the little town where the textile plants, once mighty and thriving, had all but died out and the people seemed friendly enough.

And now he not only had a new job but a new diversion: watching the uneven threesome make their mysterious trek back and forth in the night.

After a week of such perambulations, he decided to see if he could find out anything about these people without leaving his post at the store to go up and ask them himself. One morning after his shift was done and the store owners had arrived to replace him, he ambled to a diner on the same side of the highway as the hardware store to get his breakfast. He had finished his meal and was drinking a second cup of coffee when he glanced up at the waitress, a middle-aged, black-haired, pale-complexioned woman in a white apron, and asked her without prelude about the woman and her two companions and their nighttime ramblings. The woman froze at the counter a moment to consider, then shook her head slowly, absently, and said, "Sugar, I ain't got no earthly idea who or what you're talking about" and went back about her business.

"I do," said a man several seats down the counter. He was huddled up in a green plaid jacket and wore a felt hunting cap despite the morning's mildness. The remains of his breakfast lay in front of him. He had been staring down into his coffee but looked up at the inquirer and said, "Incest. That's how come she's like she is. Her mama and daddy was brothers and sisters. The boys is her brothers but by a different daddy. They're all dead now, all three of them, the mama and the two daddies." The felt-capped man paused for another sip of coffee. "Ain't no good ever comes from that kind of situation, *ever*. It not only messes up the body; it ruins the mind too." He said no more but looked down at the grease-smeared plates before him.

His questioner, the night watchman, was not quite satisfied. "But why all the traveling back and forth night after night?"

The felt-capped stranger smiled and looked back up. "Your guess is as good as mine, mister. God knows what goes on in a diseased mind like that one. What's funny is that family had money once. And a good house and a good name. Something happened. Maybe too much pride. Maybe they thought they were too good to breed outside of their own kinfolk. Kept it all in the family, so to speak." The stranger barked a laugh, then coughed, then recovered. "As far as all them night trips goes, maybe they babysitting her, them two boys. Pacifying her. Probably can't sleep. None of them. Too miserable to rest. They said she used to holler out at night. Just scream like a bobcat. That's what they say. I never heard her." He stopped to reflect. "Fine old place they have. Had. Two story. With columns and banisters and all that fancy trimming. Fine as a plantation home, which it might have been. Ain't too far from here either. Couple of miles or so from the railroad tracks. "Edith, you ever seen that house? You ever been there.?"

The woman, after a pause, shook her head, at first absently then more vehemently, as though to indicate that she wanted no part of the conversation's topic. She rubbed the counter vigorously as she answered him: "The only thing I know is, George, that nine days out of ten you full of crap, and that's because on the tenth day you ain't saying nothing!"

George, for his part, laughed into his coffee cup.

"But they carry bags," the night watchman put in. "Sometimes the bags are heavy and weigh them down. Other times they don't seem to be a burden at all. That's when they must be empty. Wonder what that's all about?"

After a moment the felt-capped stranger shook his head slowly and nodded to the waitress. "Like the lady said, mister, I aint' got no earthly idea at all about that."

He left the diner unsatisfied but more intrigued. He could not sleep that day for thinking about what the man at the counter had told him. He lay awake with all the possibilities of what went on in that once-fine house and what it meant for those three people to travel back and forth night after night, where they went, what they sought.

And later that night, alone in the darkened store, when he heard the squeaky trundling of the bizarre conveyor, the little altar, and went to the window to see the three of them, the scraggly men and the misshapen woman upon her roving pedestal, making their way through the spring darkness, he felt an almost uncontrollable urge to bolt from the store and go to them to ask them about their intentions, to satisfy his own gnawing curiosity.

Which, a week later, unable to quell his questions, is exactly what he did.

He abandoned duty, he abandoned any sort of propriety, and left the store upon first glimmer of the trio in the night. He stood at the door of the hardware store and watched their progress across the railroad tracks, moving swiftly, toward whatever destination awaited them. For a moment he was frozen, both his feet and his voice – for a moment he had considered calling out to them, "Wait for me! Please! I have so much I want to ask you!" Then he broke from the grip of his own hesitancy and sprinted across the road and up the small hill over which ran the railroad tracks.

But they were gone. Out of sight. He saw no trace of them. His pause had allowed them a getaway. Disappointed, he first thought of turning around and going back to the store but didn't. He went ahead to find them. The road by the tracks split, one half curving around a bend buttressed by a tall, white granite wall, the other running into what from the outside appeared to be a series of tree-enshrouded residences. It was the second half he picked, moving gingerly onto the sidewalk of the right side of the street. From the looks of it, even through midnight eyes, this was a poor section of town: the sidewalk broken in places into perilous chunks, some lawns untended, most houses one-story clapboard. Here and there windows burned blue and bounced with television-watching. A dog barked a single note over and over, and white street lights beat down at uneven intervals. His imagination played with him. He could see figures emerge from the shadows and come at him with hostile intent. He could sense eyes peering at him through parted curtains. Perhaps someone had already made a call to the police to report him. (But would anyone really want the police here? He doubted it.) These possibilities hurried him along. He soon found himself at the end of the block and facing an intersection. Another street of houses ran before him. To his right, the railroad tracks met a crossing. To his left, the street sloped down a hill on either side of which stood more houses. His instincts told him to go left. For the first block he found houses in the mode of the ones on the street he had just left – one-story, almost shanty-like, the yards crowded with junk, rubber tires, old bathtubs planted with flowers, children's playthings scattered about. The same lone dog-bark followed him, like some sad leitmotif connecting one forlorn street to the other. But when he crossed to the next block, it was as though he had entered another world. The houses were brick-fronted and had anchored clean, neat lawns. Gardens grew in some yards. Rose vines climbed trellises. All lights were out save for one or two burning above brick porches. He followed this block to its end. He found himself at another intersection where traffic lights signaled red and green despite there being no cars beneath them. He crossed over with a bit of quickness to his step, as though some vehicle might materialize out of the darkness and bear down on him. To his left stood Veterans' Park, and it was there he chose to go. Maybe the brothers had conveyed the woman there for some sort of perverse amusement. He entered the park through the modest tennis court and was soon absorbed in a tunnel of pine trees and maples. The walking paths had been divided into three levels, each of slightly increasing distance. He chose the lowest. It would be the easiest for anyone in their physical circumstance to travel. A lonely swing sat near the path's entrance, mute and still. Up ahead to the left huddled a gazebo; he entered it briefly but found nothing except the smell of fresh paint and a short patch of pine straw. He left it and continued on. The path encircled the park's lake. The moon threw down a cool sheen of white light on the water, and there was silence except for the occasional honking of a duck or goose. He made it to the other side: still no sign of anyone else. Another swing set appeared, just as desolate as the first, and beside it were a slide, a sandbox, and some monkey bars. For a moment a vision, both comic and terrible, appeared to him of the woman attempting to maneuver the bars with her armless hands, her miniature torso swinging back and forth wildly. But no one was there. Not a soul.

    He completed the path and ended up where he began, at the tennis court. He was a young man but one with a bit of a paunch and a habit for tobacco. He had winded himself with the walk and took a few moments to recover before heading back to the hardware store. He experienced a second wave of exhaustion by the time he made it to the railroad tracks and leaned against a stop sign. Not more than a moment passed before he heard a noise behind him. He turned. There they were, the three of them, a human juggernaut: one brother pushing the woman on her pedestal, the other acting as a kind of guide, a clearer of the path before them. They flashed past him, moving quickly over the train tracks. They spoke to each other, the men anyway, but their words were indecipherable. They laughed but never acknowledged him. The guiding brother held the same burlap sack which looked heavy and bumped against his thigh.

A Plinth of Night

He stepped away from the stop sign, as though he might go in pursuit of them. "Hey!" he called after them. "Wait!" But they didn't. They continued on down the road, lit up occasionally by a random street light, until darkness swallowed them up completely.

The following night he waited for them at the stop sign, but they did not appear until after he had given up and retreated to the store. The night after that he watched from the store window until they appeared; then he went after them. They moved so fast! It wasn't long before he lost sight of them but continued on anyway. He arrived at the same intersection he had come to two nights earlier. This time he did not turn left or right but moved straight ahead, crossing the street into a short block of one-story, white-washed houses with low roofs and miniscule lawns, past a broad brick and wood building housing a roofing outfit, then past a smaller building where gravestones were sold, stopping, finally and appropriately, at a cemetery elevated above the street and encased by a cement wall topped by wrought-iron railings.

Right away he could hear the sounds of voices and labor: the rhythmic rise and fall of something hard and solid hitting the ground repeatedly. They were here. He knew it and raced up the sidewalk to level ground to have a look, to confirm his instinct. Maybe fifty feet away, over the tops of headstones and special, more elaborate markers decorated with marble seraphim and praying hands, he could make the three of them out in the dark. Indeed one of the brothers was using an instrument, a pickaxe or shovel, to assault a gravesite while the other looked on. The woman, on her pedestal, watched as well and could herself have been mistaken for a marble monument among so many others. She had the same kind of stilted regality.

He watched them only a minute or so more. A panic seized his whole body and made his heart accelerate. Graverobbing. They were graverobbers. And what if they were caught and he near them, so close as to be considered an accomplice? He rushed away from the cemetery, back down the cement sidewalk, retracing his steps until he found himself back at the stop sign at the railroad crossing, at first too preoccupied with catching his breath to notice that the hardware store across the road was lit up bright as day and a pick-up truck sat in front of it, shiny from the lights inside. Another wave of panic refueled his oxygen. He took off across the road at a sprint.

Mr. Alexander, one of the two brothers who owned the store, sat waiting for him in a hardback chair at the front of the store, near a panel of washers and screws. He was smoking a cigarette, flicking the ashes into a Styrofoam cup. Directly over his head perched a red-lettered NO SMOKING notice. He stared straight at his night watchman like a father waiting for a child who has broken curfew.

"Sometimes I can't sleep," he began slowly. He was a medium-sized, white-haired in his late fifties wearing silver eyeglasses that caught glints from the store's fluorescent lighting. "Worrying about everything. This business mainly. Times ain't good for nobody. And people breaking in here don't help none." He took another drag and sighed out the smoke. "So where was you tonight? Out chasing tail?" He laughed and coughed and took a moment to recover. "Ain't what we paying you for. Paying you to stay here and keep a watch on things. Instead you left it wide open for anybody to come in and pick it off. Ah Lord." He sighed, sucked in more smoke, let it go. "Looks like we just going to have to break down and put in one of them surveillance systems. And they cost out the wazoo too. But the ain't ways ain't working no more. People don't take pride in a job no more, when they ought to count theirselves lucky to have one."

So he left the store just before dawn, newly unemployed, and went back to his room and lay on his bed in his same clothes. Mr. Alexander's insomnia proved contagious. But he didn't worry about losing his job. Instead his mind buzzed with questions about the three siblings and with the image of the brother with the implement into the ground. For what reason? They behaved brazenly about it, not caring who might come upon them. Whatever it was they sought in the ground, more than likely it was that they carried home in the sack. Could they be looking for trinkets, valuable things buried with the dead that they could sell? Was this their livelihood following the ruin of their family and their home? He could go back to the cemetery and confront them, but he didn't like the idea. It posed too much danger. The best thing would be to go to the house itself —while they were out doing their midnight scavenging – to see what he could find. He wouldn't be satisfied until then.

That night he waited for them to pass. He stood in the shadows not too far from his former place of employment, the hardware store, and watched the three of them go off to their dark ramblings, their scrounging, whatever it was that they planned to do that night. Then he headed in the opposite direction, fleet-footed, not knowing how much time he had, looking for Adeline Road where, according to George, the felt hat-wearing diner, the strange family still kept its homestead. It was a foolish search. The night was huge and black and nearly moonless. He had no idea where he was going. He didn't know the town well enough. It was too late to go to someone to ask directions. He stumbled and fumbled into dead ends and cul-de-sacs. In some places he encountered nothing but brush or intimidating pine tree stands and /or ditches that yawned wide from the road and would swallow a man whole. It was then he felt an almost childish panic at being lost. He had to choke back an urge to holler or cry. And then he took off, scrambling to wherever he could see lights in household windows. His footsteps awakened an untethered, hostile dog. The dog, a mere frantic, feral shape in the dark, chased him for blocks and yards before it quit him and went back home, which it knew through instinct alone and nothing else. But this encounter proved fortuitous for the man; at the end of it, he stood at the entrance to Adeline Road. A green street sign, which he could barely make out in the poor night light, verified the fact.

From what he could see, however, Adeline Road was a virtual jungle. Bramble covered both sides of the road. The pines and oaks were nearly swallowed up in kudzu grass. And there were only the faintest demarcations of a path cutting through the chaos. No house lights shone. There were no street lamps. He would have to pick his way carefully up Adeline to find what he sought – the house of the woman on the plinth.

He went forward slowly, putting his foot down with the constant apprehension that he might step upon something alive which would not forgive him the offense. Tree frogs sang all around with throats hot and crusty, suddenly ceasing before resuming their piercing dirge. Something he could not see touched his face and brushed through his hair. Spider web. From where it hung he didn't know. He just beat it away from his head as best he could and rubbed off the remains on the back of his pants. He must have gone three dozen feet or more before an old Spanish style villa house appeared on his right, its columns sloping, its overall bone-whiteness lighting up the night. This could not be the house he was seeking. He knew it. It was one-story for one thing. For another, it did not have the dignity of the aristocratic, not even faded aristocracy. There was something loose and tawdry about its structure and its appearance on Adeline, exotic and tasteless, and he saw no need to hike up the driveway that wound down from the house's porch to explore it. So he moved on.

When he had gone what he estimated to be a whole mile, the moon broke through the black clouds, leaving them ragged and tawdry, and flooded the land with fluorescent illumination. Everything had a stark, ghostly confusion about it, as though a cataract had dropped over both his eyes. He waited a moment for his vision to adjust to the this new light, and when it did he became excited, for he was sure he saw up ahead a chimney stack peering over a line of pine trees. He picked up his walking pace to a near-trot in the direction of this new sight, northwest, where it rested on a slight incline. As he got closer, more details emerged coyly through the trees' obstruction, revealing, in pieces at least, a house still grand in the judgment of the late-night darkness. And when he came to the threshold of the grounds proper, he stopped and studied the edifice in front of him. It indeed stood two stories and had a definite air of importance around it, even with no lights shining in the now dead, moon-blinded windows. He had expected a wraparound porch, a gallery of some kind, extending beyond the front door and stretching around both sides of the house. That was the way he pictured all such homes in the country South. But no such thing existed here. And when he thought upon the history of the family that owned it, of what he had been told of its character, the absence of such a free, open space made sense. He could not exactly envision them as the kind of people who would while away the sweltering hours outside with small talk and pleasant anecdotes. Instead there was a small porch offset on either side by long, wide windows now muffled by moonshine. Two more such windows stood on the second story. The roof was gabled and ended in the long gray finger of the chimney.

So there the house stood. He had no doubt of it. But why had he come to it? What did he hope to find? He wasn't sure exactly: an answer, he supposed, to what that woman and her two brothers meant, if they meant anything at all. But he would find nothing just standing there, so he edged closer to the house, wading almost through the high-grown sedge and weeds, until he reached the front porch. Would the three of them be so conscious, so careful as to lock the front door? For some reason he thought not but was proven wrong when he tried it. It stood solid against his efforts to open it. This disappointed him. He walked to the far end of the porch and peered out into the night but saw nothing except more moon-bathed trees and grass. He left the porch and stalked around the house's left flank but again saw nothing of promise as far as an entry into the house. He could smash one of the windows and get in that way, but for some reason he rejected that solution (he wanted it to be *easy* so no one would find a trace of his having been there) and moved on to the back of the house, where right away the moon pointed out something to him: an old fashioned ground door cellar peeping out through the grasses. A rusty lock secured it closed, of course, but at this point of desperation and curiosity he lost all sense of propriety and sought something with which to break the hasp. He hunted the dark, overgrown yard until he came upon a piece of stone, a rock, that took both his hands to hold and carried it back to the cellar door.

He dropped it again and again until he heard the lock break. Then he yanked aside both panels of the door and stared down into the black hole. The moon traveled only so far down the stone steps then gave out. He went down the steps, and when there was no more moon, he brought out his cigarette lighter and flicked a flame into life. It gave off very little light, certainly not enough to make a safe trip around the unknown cellar. Still he shone it round and could make out the brick walls and cement floor. He took diffident steps, and the farther in he got, the deeper, a cacophony of odors met him: must, damp, rot, and others which to him had an industrialized tint. He became so absorbed in his revulsion to these smells and in trying to differentiate their individual scents, he lost mind of his walking and tripped on some inconsistency in the floor. Losing his balance, he flung the lighter into the darkness and lost it. He braced himself against the wall and stared back at the patch of moonlight so many feet away now. He thought a moment of going back and leaving the house but instead moved ahead, patting the wooden rafters of the ceiling with both his hands in hopes of coming upon a light switch or dangling chain attached to a light bulb.

And then it happened: he put his foot down where there was no more ground to meet him. He dropped what must at least have been five feet and remained so crouched on solid concrete flooring as pain seared his joints. He stood right away, as though to protect himself from humiliation more than pain, but his knees sagged from their new wound and he had to grab onto the wall to keep from falling again. After a moment of steadiness, he reached above his head once more to hunt for a light and found it this time; a chain descended from the ceiling. He gave it a hard yank. A single, bare, dirty bulb popped into white, garish life and showed him the cement shelf off which he had just fallen. It also showed him the narrow cubicle in which he stood, impenetrable except for the wooden door that stood in front of him. Maybe one or two other grown men could have fit into the space at the same time. The shock of having fallen wore off, replaced by growing panic and a renewed pain in his knees. In fact, they felt as though they had been set on fire, and he leaned on the floor to keep from falling again. Suddenly the secrets of the house did not matter as much to him. All he wanted now was to leave the place. But he wasn't sure he could clamber back up the shelf and return the way he had come. His hands smarted fiercely and his knees hurt more by the minute. He was sure that if he looked down he would find them stained through his pants with blood. In fact, he could feel such wetness without looking or touching. Maybe he had broken something. All he knew was he wished he could sit down a moment and see how much strength he could recover before carrying on. It would be best to stumble through a passage in the house on the way out, if such passage existed, and to use his arms to grab onto things should his legs fail him.

The door on which he propped himself stood between him and possible freedom, but he felt sure it was locked and was surprised to find it give way to the shove of his shoulder. He found more darkness on the other side of the door and smacked the inside of a wall, nervously trying to find a light. His hand came upon a conventional wall switch and he flipped it. The room lit up in a dead-white light, the light of translucent flesh, but he had no idea what he was staring at. It was a puzzle, a maze that took a few moments to sort through and bring into any kind of order.

What he noticed first was a door parallel to the one in which he stood, some ten feet or so away. Between him and it stood an old rickety wooden table whose blue paint peeled badly and left flakes on the hard floor. On top of it lay a set of men's clothing, a dark suit consisting of coat and pants and black shoes. After staring at it a moment and adjusting to its presence in the unreliable light, he realized someone was in the clothes and lying on his side as though taking a nap. He grew quickly heartened at the appearance of another human being. "Hello!" he shouted and lunged into the room to make acquaintance, possibly to establish alliance. But he fooled himself. His weak knees gave and he fell. He grabbed the edge of the table and took the whole thing to the floor with him. The table fell upon him, as did the man on it. "I'm sorry!" he hollered, but when he opened his eyes he found himself staring not into the face of a newly-awakened man but of someone, *something* that had ranged far beyond sleep into another country altogether. It was hardly a human face at all anymore: some flesh remained, now hanging inches from him in fetid strips like pieces of Spanish moss and with the same odor, but the eyes were gone and mostly a skull grinned down at him; the hands had grown skeletal as well.

He screamed and heaved the body off him and attempted to rise from the floor. Pain battered his legs fiercely, though, and he wound up back on the floor. He took this interval of helplessness to make inventory of the rest of the room, and what he saw sickened him and made him cry out a second time. On wooden shelves one might have found in any perfectly normal home rest bones, long and short, leg bones, arm bones, hip bones, and at least one fully intact rib cage, washed cleaned and as bright and shiny as something artificial purchased in a store. Cabinets stood open above the shelves and revealed skulls stacked one upon the other as though they had been dinnerware. They too had been scrubbed to a vivid whiteness, made clean from anything rotted. And pervading everything was that industrial scent. Formaldehyde? Rat poison? He wasn't sure. He moved to try to stand again, but his legs wouldn't have it – he was sure now he had broken something – and he returned to the floor, not sure how he would escape. He propped himself on an elbow and stared at the unopened door, sure it was his means of leaving, if only he could get to it. He could crawl, he supposed, then pictured himself in such a hapless effort and abandoned it.

Then, as though he willed it, as though his need had legs and hands of its own, the door swung open in a long, slow arc. Darkness stood behind the door and silence too, and it was the silence he dreaded more.

"Hello?" he called out. "Is anyone there? Help me please!?"

A moment of further silence followed his plea, and then came a quiet squeaking which seemed to emanate from far away and to take forever to culminate. When it did, the doorway was filled with a presence that was both strange to him and familiar. From his panic it took him a moment to realize who it was: the woman on the plinth, the partial human being perched on her ambulatory pedestal. He could ignore the absence of her limbs concealed by short, flounced sleeves and a hemline that left a small crinoline pool around her waist. Her face commanded his attention, framed in duplicate waves of soft white hair. She stared down at him with what was clearly anger but which paled her face further instead of reddening it. She moved her lips vehemently, though no sound came from them.

"I'm sorry," he said to her. "I know I shouldn't be here, but..." He could not finish. He did not know why he was there, and he felt whatever answer he might offer would not satisfy her. And the woman didn't seem to care. She just continued to speak silently, as though pronouncing an incantation over him.

He reached up to her beseechingly and was so intent on winning her mercy, he did not hear the footsteps of the two brothers, who seemed to have come from out of nowhere. He wasn't aware of them at all until they land hands on him and lifted him from the floor and held him against themselves, giving off the stench of dirt and flesh and formaldehyde. They twisted his neck so that he faced the ceiling, but out of the corner of his eyes he could see their wild, white grins. They spoke indecipherable words to him and to each other and grunted and laughed.

"Please!" he managed to get out, and that was when one of the brothers closed a rag doused with something potent-smelling over his face, and he almost instantly lost all panic and concern and the very room itself.

It was an unusual summer for the little town, a place not used to startling events.

First came the reports of the graverobbings, the seemingly random violation of resting places at various cemeteries around town. For about a three week period someone had disrupted gravesites, opening the caskets, removing corpses, taking things from them – parts of the remains, not any jewelry or other such valuables – but bones. Skulls were missing, as were leg and arm bones and even ribcages. It was a ghastly occurrence, of course, and had the townspeople speaking of it in varying tones of disbelief and disgust. Some even joked about it: "Well, at least they're robbin' the dead and not the livin.' That leaves me out!" But when it was clear these morbid "visitations" had become epidemic, and the police had begun a more rigorous patrol of the cemeteries, they stopped.

Not long after this incident, another oddity caught the attention of the townspeople: the appearance, in full daylight and in conspicuous places, of a rather bizarre quartet: three men and woman. They seemed to burst out of thin air, just to be there when only seconds ago they hadn't been. They were noisy and rowdy, talking and laughing at such volume as to draw attention, but no one ever understood the subjects of their conversations or the punchlines of their jokes. It was almost as though they had their own language. Two of the men, lean, lanky, and perpetually unshaven, were brothers, and the woman, an albino missing both her arms and legs, was their sister. Theirs was an irredeemably ugly story and not recounted except by those who enjoyed the exploitation of the unfortunate. The woman's condition had resulted from the copulation between a brother and sister, occupants of a fine old restored plantation home on the town's outskirts and owners of a name that once commanded respect and even affection. How they had come to such calamity never became clear. There were contradicting stories of jealousy and greed and attempts to keep the sister from leaving the homestead for good.

Because of her infirmity, the woman had to be pushed from place to place by one of the brothers on a makeshift carriage, almost like a baby stroller, with a flat surface on which she sat, pale and still, like some damaged work of sculpture – as did the third man. He too lacked extremities, and he too was conveyed by a brother on a contraption similar to the woman's. No one knew who he was though. A missing brother? Someone who up to then they had successfully kept from public view? He had come from nowhere but fit right in with his three companions. From time to time, as they rushed past business fronts or down the streets of the town center, he could be seen flashing a smile at something said by the man pushing him. There was even speculation that he and the woman, impossible and grotesque as it might seem, might be involved in a romantic liaison. They certainly looked like a couple.

Some wanted to find out for sure. They even had the audacity to suggest going up to this "family" and asking point-blank what the state of the relations were. But invariably they backed down, realizing it was best just to let them be.

Landscape

The sun, a single red eye, burnt what was left of the earth, holding everything beneath it in a heavy, never-dimming glare. It never left the sky, not even in those hours once reserved for night and the stars.

The land lay red and uneven under it like flayed flesh, gorges deep and hills steep. Almost nothing remained, all flora and fauna dried to dust and indistinguishable from the dirt already there, water reduced to trickles, air clogged with the stench of the dead.

Birds, fish, and anything on four legs, even the most-lowly crawling ant or roach, had long disappeared, victims of heat and dissolution.

It was more than a desert. It was Hell raised to the level of an earthly horizon.

All one could see through the dense, dusty glare was a stack of triangular oddities, books that had once been designated when language had use and a scant few could read them: hard-backed and leather-bound, containing all that had once been cherished: story, song, law, history, mathematics, science, theology.... No other evidence existed of these aspirations. A hapless soul had abandoned them there in child-like hope then disappeared into anonymity.

Then *they* came.

The marauders, man and animal conjoined, naked, tattooed, pierced, eyes dead, mouths full of their own blood, their own flesh. At times, bumping against each other, they gave the impression of being one thing, a single monstrosity; then, parting again, they revealed their individual obscenities. They tore across the hot, dead, powdery plain in a pack, yapping at each other, moving their red mouths but saying nothing, yelling and bellowing, snapping like crazed dogs after fleshless bones.

They had come from elsewhere, nowhere now, having dismantled the temples, torn down the monuments, crashed the statues, erased the noble names, obliterated anything beautiful and true with their bile, their blood, their feces.

Even in the throes of their chaos, they spotted the small tower of books, as a leopard catches a glimpse of a hapless gazelle. The scent of authenticity reached them and nauseated them further, as blood is said to madden the maws of dogs and turn them into killers. They growled, they shouted, they fought each other for the opportunity to topple the tower. They fell upon the books and rent them into pieces, flinging the pages into the hot glare of the pitiless sun. They shoved pages into their mouths and regurgitated them at once, unable to digest what they could not understand. Shakespeare sickened them, as did Plato, as did Kant, as did Euclid, as did Livy, as did all the others who had written of what it had once meant to be human. They destroyed the books and left the remains to the whim of the sand and sun.

And moved on. They left, blindly, the taste for destruction still potent in their noses, their mouths, towards what else they must devour.

About the Author

RANDALL "RANDY" IVEY is a lifelong South Carolinian who has taught at the University of South Carolina in his native Union for thirty-four years. On nine different occasions, he has been named the institution's "Distinguished Teacher of the Year." He also directs the university's annual Upcountry Literary Festival, a gathering of some of the South's finest writers, musicians, and storytellers.

His previous books include three other books of stories (including *A New England Romance and Other Southern Stories*, Green Altar Books first publication), three novels (two under a pseudonym), and a book for children. He has published more than two hundred stories, poems, essays, and reviews in journals, magazines, newspapers, anthologies, and websites throughout the United States and in the United Kingdom.

He is currently researching a biography of his fellow Union Countian William "Singing Billy" Walker, the nineteenth-century composer, arranger, and song-catcher world-renowned for his version of "Amazing Grace."

Randall Ivey

Available From Green Altar Books

If you enjoyed this book, perhaps some of our other titles will pique your interest. The following titles are now available for your reading pleasure... Enjoy!

Green Altar Books
Shotwell Publishing

Green Altar (Literary Imprint)

Catharine Brosman
An Aesthetic Education and Other Stories (2nd Ed)

Chained Tree, Chained Owls: Poems

Aerosols and Other Poems

Randall Ivey
A New England Romance: And Other Southern Stories

Suzanne Johnson
Maxcy Gregg's Sporting Journals 1842-1858

James E. Kibler, Jr.
Tiller : Claybank County Series, Vol. 4

The Gentler Gamester

In the Deep Heart's Core: Poems of Tribute and Remembrance (forthcoming)

Thomas Moore
A Fatal Mercy: The Man Who Lost The Civil War

Perrin Lovett
The Substitute, Tom Ironsides 1

Karen Stokes
Belles

Carolina Twilight

Honor in the Dust

The Immortals

The Soldier's Ghost: A Tale of Charleston

William Thomas
Runaway Haley: An Imagined Family Saga

The Field of Justice: Moonshine and Murder in North Georgia

Gold-Bug
(Mystery & Suspense Imprint)

Brandi Perry
Splintered: A New Orleans Tale

Martin Wilson
To Jekyll and Hide

www.ingramcontent.com/pod-product-compliance
Ingram Content Group UK Ltd.
Pitfield, Milton Keynes, MK11 3LW, UK
UKHW021326180426
11947UKWH00017B/1473